About the author

Robert Dickinson lives in Brighton and is the author of two volumes of poetry, *Micrographia* and *Szyzgy* (with Andrew Dilger), a comedy drama, *Murder's Last Case*, and the libretto for Joby Talbot's choral work *Path of Miracles*. *The Noise of Strangers* is his first novel.

the noise of strangers

Robert Dickinson

Myriad Editions

First published in 2010 by
Myriad Editions
59 Lansdowne Place
Brighton BN3 1FL

www.MyriadEditions.com

1 3 5 7 9 10 8 6 4 2

A CIP catalogue record for this book is available from the
British Library.

ISBN: 978-0-9562515-1-0

Printed on FSC-accredited paper by
CPI Antony Rowe, Chippenham, UK.

FSC
Mixed Sources
Product group from well-managed
forests and other controlled sources
Cert no. SGS-COC-2953
www.fsc.org
© 1996 Forest Stewardship Council

*The city of confusion is broken down: every house is shut
up, that no man may come in.*
*There is a crying for wine in the streets; all joy is
darkened, the mirth of the land is gone.*
*In the city is left desolation, and the gate is smitten with
destruction.*
*From the uttermost parts of the earth have we heard
songs, even glory to the righteous. But I said, My
leanness, my leanness, woe unto me! the treacherous
dealers have dealt treacherously; yea, the treacherous
dealers have dealt very treacherously.*
*Fear, and the pit, and the snare are upon thee, O
inhabitant of the earth.*
*The earth is utterly broken down, the earth is clean
dissolved, the earth is moved exceedingly.*

WHAT CAN BE DONE?

PRAYER MEETING

*Thou shalt bring down the noise of strangers, as the heat
in a dry place; even the heat with the shadow of a cloud.*

All Saints Church, 6.00 pm–8.30 pm
(No firearms)

Denise

Denise hated the drive home. At night, driving across town was as bad as driving through the countryside. Once through the security gate at the bottom of Southover Street the only visible lights were the squatters' campfires on the Level. Except at a checkpoint or guard post the roads would be black, the pavements lost in shadow, with only the occasional candle in an upstairs window to show they were passing houses where people lived. Their own house was only a few miles away, but the journey always inspired the same nausea.

And then there was Jack. 'This is the kind of nonsense I mean.' Denise didn't know what he was talking about. 'I mean, this can add, what, ten minutes to the journey.'

She realised he was talking about the new one-way system. 'You can't complain,' she said, although she knew he always would. 'You designed it.'

Jack tutted and turned right, heading towards the Lewes Road. 'Actually, this one was Alan's.'

'But you approved it.'

'That's not the point. Oh, bloody hell.' He braked

3

sharply. At the top of the Level the traffic lights were still working, and showed red. He stopped, even though it was after midnight and there were no other cars on the road. Denise said nothing. The way Jack followed rules when there was no need was one of the things they argued about. Jack would say that he was maintaining standards, setting an example. Denise thought it was safer to keep moving.

The squatters worried her. She knew they were harmless, that they would drink their moonshine, sing their hymns, and then wait, as they did every night, for the end of the world. In the morning T & E would drive them back into the slums around Russell Street, where they would sit on the pavements until it was dark enough for them to return, when they would once again drink their moonshine and sing their hymns. Denise was not scared of the squatters themselves: what made her uneasy was what they represented. She thought she could remember a time when, except for a few known tramps, the Level was empty at night.

'Look at them.' Jack glared at the campfires. 'Useless scum.' His anger was at more than the squatters or the one-way system, but Denise was too tired to care about its real object. Jack was always angry at something. Sometimes he pretended it was amusement or scorn or principled outrage; for now it was just anger.

The lights changed. He headed towards London Road, passing the boarded-up windows of Baker Street. 'I suppose you'd prefer it if we lived in Hanover.'

'You know I would.' Hanover was something else they argued about. It was the ward where, somehow, everybody they knew lived. At least once a week they would make this journey to some dinner party or other. 'You have to admit it would be more convenient.' Denise could have said more but was distracted by the stray dogs prowling outside the shell of the old Co-op building. There was supposed to be a nest of them, if that was the word, in the basement. Supposed to be: one of the rumours that, in this town, passed for knowledge. The council had plans for the building: another depot for Transport and Environment, or a holding centre for Welfare – anything to stop the rot spreading north from the Russell Street slums. 'At least we could walk home afterwards,' she offered. 'You'd be able to drink.' And she would need to drink less.

'The houses are too small.' Jack frowned into his rear-view mirror. 'And we'd have to listen to Alan and Margaret arguing every night.'

The tiredness was like a weight behind her eyes. Where did he get this idea? 'Alan and Margaret don't argue.'

'No?' He took a left up New England Road, towards the looming Victorian viaduct on which Denise could remember having once seen a train. She'd been a child; it might have been the first train she'd seen, though sometimes she wondered if she'd seen it at all, or simply been told about it so often she now believed she had. She wondered if dwelling on this kind of uncertainty was a sign of age. Or was it the wine? There had been seven people and five bottles of wine; Siobhan hadn't drunk any, Jack had nursed the same half-glass the whole evening, Alan and Margaret and Tim and Louise … She made the familiar, depressing calculations. Jack sighed through clenched teeth. 'Did you see that graffiti? Couldn't even spell Henderson properly.' Denise looked, but the words were behind them now, and the walls ahead were covered with posters bearing a cross, the sign of the Helmstone mission. There were no words, but then most of the Helmstoners couldn't read, and weren't so different from the squatters on the open ground. They didn't drink, lived in houses and sang different hymns, and most of them had low-level council jobs, but they waited for the end of the world as fervently as any of the derelicts on the Level. Denise almost envied them their hope. She knew the world was not going to end: it would grind on and on until they and all their dismissive taxonomy (Stoner, Scoomer, squatter, scum) were dead and forgotten. 'And how can you say they don't argue?' Jack asked. Denise forced herself to concentrate: he was still talking about Alan and Margaret. 'They barely spoke to each other.'

'That's not the same as arguing.'

'So you think they're happy?'

'I don't know. But they don't argue.' Denise wondered how Jack could be so wrong. Alan and Margaret were too intent on presenting themselves as a successful couple to disagree in front of outsiders. 'And I don't know where you've got the idea they do.'

'Don't you?' They stopped for more lights. Again there was no other traffic in any direction. 'For crying out loud. This is the kind of thing I mean.' This time she couldn't tell what he was talking about: the pointless lights or her lack of perception, or something else he expected her to guess. His anger was indiscriminate. He turned to her. 'Alan can be such a bastard. The way he carries on with Louise. And Margaret is sitting right there.'

'Tim doesn't seem to mind.'

'Tim doesn't seem to notice. Here's Alan, flirting outrageously with his wife, and he's – I don't know what he's doing.'

'Lights.'

'Right.' He eased across the junction, where, surprisingly, more traffic had appeared: two dirty white Fiats, Scoomer cars, spluttering up from the other direction. The passenger of one was leaning from his window, as if trying to climb out. He shouted at them and waved, laughing. Both cars weaved as they headed away.

'Careful,' Denise said.

'They weren't a problem.' Jack, for once, sounded tolerant. 'They're gone now.'

Denise couldn't relax until the cars were out of sight. 'They're dangerous because they don't care. Henderson voters.'

'If they're Scoomers they're Labour. Besides, I don't think they were old enough to vote.' Jack checked the rear view again. He might have pretended to be unconcerned, but he didn't want those cars to turn round either. They drove on for a few seconds without talking. Then Jack sighed. 'Alan is such a bastard.' So he was back on that hobby horse. 'That's *why* I was talking to him, to keep him away from Louise. I mean, do you think I want to talk about one-way systems all night? I get enough of them at work.'

'I get enough of them at home.'

'I'm sorry. Sorry. It's just such a big deal at the moment. Force the motorists on to the toll roads. Maximise the income.'

'That's Henderson's thing, isn't it? Abolish the toll roads.'

'Henderson's a nobody.' Prestonville Road was empty. Jack, she noticed, was still checking his rear view. There were stories of children in stolen cars driving without lights, for fun. It was supposed to be called 'blinding'. You didn't see them until it was too late. Another rumour that passed for fact. 'He'll never win anything. And even if he did he wouldn't do it.' Jack's voice softened to resigned bitterness. 'Not when he finds out how much money it makes.'

'Jack, I've heard enough about it for one night. It wasn't supposed to be a summit meeting. Alan and Margaret invited us there to eat.'

'I know, I know ...' They slowed at the foot of the hill. A Bentley with an escort of four motorcycles swept past them. 'Councillor Goss.' Jack narrowed his eyes. 'Where's he been this time of night?'

'Don't ask me.'

'I thought Audit knew everybody's dirty little secrets.'

'Probably a dinner party. Just like us.'

'Councillor Goss? I doubt it.' The lights changed. Jack took a right. 'Even so ...'

'This isn't the way.'

'I know.'

'So what are you doing?' Denise put her hands on the dashboard as if bracing herself for a sudden stop. 'You're not following him, are you?'

Jack grinned at her. It was the first time he'd smiled the whole evening. 'If he's going through the Ditchling Road toll I can tailgate, and avoid Preston Road.'

'You'll add ten minutes to our journey to save five pounds?'

'Seven minutes. And every little helps.' They'd caught up with the councillor's motorcade. Jack slowed to match its pace. One of the motorcyclists glanced back, but otherwise they were ignored; the benefit of having a good car with a blue council badge in the windscreen. Jack bit his lower lip, a sign of concentration. 'I thought you'd appreciate that, being in Audit.'

'Audit isn't about money.'

'Everything is about money.' He glanced in the rear view. 'Looks like somebody else has the same idea.'

She turned. Another car was coming up behind them, headlights full on. 'Scoomers,' she said. 'What are they doing here?'

'You can't say they're Scoomers just because it's a Fiat.'

'It's a good rule of thumb. Shit, they're not slowing down.' Famous last words, she thought: it would be just my luck … When it was inches away the car swerved, overtaking them and the motorcade. 'Maniac,' she said – or possibly only thought. For a moment she wasn't sure.

'Close,' Jack said.

'You should have gone the usual way. This road's a menace.'

'And paid the Preston Road toll? He missed us, didn't he?' He grinned again. Yes, he was amused by her terror. It probably made him feel manly. 'So, what were you and Margaret talking about all evening? Her miserable marriage?'

'Margaret and Alan aren't married.'

'You know what I mean.'

'Actually we were talking about Doug and Sarah.'

Jack kept his eyes on the road ahead. 'I think that counts as talking about her miserable marriage by proxy.'

The way he said *I think that counts* made her head ache. There were times when talking to Jack was like banging your shin against a familiar piece of furniture. You knew it was there and were still surprised it could make you wince. 'Doug and Sarah aren't unhappy. As far as anybody knows.'

'No.' Jack gave the mirthless smile that usually preceded a witticism. 'But I sometimes believe you lot think they ought to be.'

You lot: the women. 'That's not fair.'

'But you're always wondering how Sarah ended up with someone like Doug.'

'You have to admit it was unexpected.'

'Doesn't mean it was wrong.' Now he was disagreeing with her for the sake of it. 'I know he doesn't have our education. But you talk about him as if he were a Scoomer.'

'So do you, half the time. Besides, he's a Henderson voter.'

'Rubbish.' He glanced at her, suddenly concerned. 'Or do you know something?'

'That's what Sarah says.' She corrected herself. 'That's what Margaret says Sarah says.'

'Then she should leave him. But she won't because he isn't. Here we go.' Ahead of them they could see the barrier beginning to rise. Jack concentrated on maintaining his distance from the motorcade. 'See? That's five pounds saved.'

'I hate going through these.' Denise stared dead ahead as they passed under the barrier. Two guards stood to awkward attention beside the booth, their rifles slung over their shoulders, their faces carefully blank beneath their uniform caps. 'They worry me,' she said, seconds later, when the barrier was down behind them. 'I always think one of them is about to crack up and start shooting at people.'

'You say that every time. There are vetting procedures, you know.' He slowed, allowing the motorcade to pull away. 'Thank you, Councillor Goss. And now ...' He had no sooner turned off the road than she heard horns blaring behind them, then a screech and metal crashing into metal, followed a moment later by what sounded like a second, heavier collision.

Jack swore. Denise looked back, but couldn't see anything. 'Don't stop.'

But Jack had already stopped and was reversing back down the street. In the upper windows lights were starting to appear. 'I'm only going to have to deal with this in the morning. I might as well see what it is now.'

'Yes, in the morning ...' There were four motorcyclists – council officials – already at the scene. It was their job to handle this kind of incident. 'What difference can you make now? You can deal with it in the morning ...'

Jack wasn't listening. He reversed until they were back on Ditchling Road.

The first thing Denise saw, two or three hundred yards ahead of the junction, was a bright orange flare behind a barricade, as if a civic bonfire had been pitched incongruously in the middle of the dark street. She couldn't see the councillor's Bentley. Had it turned off the road? Had the noise they heard been caused by other cars? Then she realised the barricade *was* the Bentley, thrown on to its side, its roof towards them. As her eyes adjusted she could make out two of the motorbikes lying in the road beside it. One of the riders was leaning against a post and tugging frantically at his helmet as if he thought it was on fire. He seemed to be the only person on the street. She couldn't see the rider of the other motorbike, and was surprised how quiet everything seemed. She could hear nothing other than the sound of their own engine: no cries for help, no other cars. The flames seemed to be burning silently, as if they were much further away than they looked. As Jack turned the car to face them they seemed to die down. Denise watched them, fascinated despite herself. Suddenly the rider staggered forward, bent at the waist. He pulled off his helmet as if he had finally remembered how to loosen the strap, then threw it into the gutter with what looked like disgust. He walked unsteadily towards the upturned car. 'You've seen it,' Denise said. 'Now go.'

'They may need help.'

'What can you do? They're not your responsibility.'

'If it's not mine …'

Jack straightened the car. Immediately, Denise heard a popping sound that seemed to come from nowhere in particular. She thought they had driven over something, but then Jack swore. He braked and turned so sharply they jolted against the kerb.

The impact made her nauseous. She clutched the dashboard as he ground them through another wrenching turn. 'What was that?'

'It wasn't the engine.'

She swallowed hard. It had sounded too light for gunfire, unless it was from a sidearm: a bodyguard, terrified and in shock, firing at anything that moved. 'Are you sure?'

'No.' His sense of their danger was finally stronger than his work ethic. 'But I'm not staying to find out.'

They drove in silence for the next two streets. Denise clenched her teeth and took deep breaths and gradually felt better. From far off, and seemingly from different directions, came the sound of sirens. Jack said, 'This is going to be a headache tomorrow. If we have to close that road ...'

The job again. She said: 'What about Goss?'

'He's not my responsibility. The road is.' His hands drummed the steering wheel, as if trying to dislodge a thought. 'Shit. I need to talk to Alan.'

They reached their street. The security guard (Paul? Oscar?) let them through the gate after no more than a glance. He seemed to be listening to the noise of the sirens as raptly as a Helmstoner listened to hymns.

Jack eased their car into their allotted space and stopped the engine. Normally he would sigh and sit for a second or two. Now he jumped out of the car and skipped across the pavement as if he thought they were under fire. Denise hadn't seen him move as quickly in years. He was at their building before she could get out of the car. By the time she reached the security grille he had already unlocked the street door and was heading towards the staircase. Ignoring the lift, he bounded up the stairs with Denise clattering unsteadily behind him. When she reached the flat he was already standing by the phone. 'Let's hope the lines are working tonight.' He was panting from the exertion.

She limped behind him. 'What are you doing?'

He picked up the receiver and started to dial. 'I'm letting Alan know.'

'Can't it wait until the morning?'

'It's going to be a lot of work. We'll need to start as

early as possible.' He placed the receiver to his ear and listened intently.

'It's two in the morning.' But it was useless talking to Jack when he was in this kind of mood.

'Alan? It's Jack. We've just got in. You heard it? Yes, we saw it. You're not going to believe this ...'

She went to the bathroom and threw up with a sudden violence. Her mouth was filled with the taste of red wine. She drank a glass of water and tried not to think about what she'd just seen, but couldn't. For Jack, it was all a matter of one-way systems, but if Councillor Goss had been in that car then there were political ramifications and that would matter to Audit because everything, in the end, mattered to Audit.

It could wait until Monday morning. For now she was tired and her head ached. She wiped her mouth as the cistern refilled. When she came out of the room Jack was still on the phone, talking.

Is this thing working?

Yes. Can't you hear?

That buzzing?

What? I'm sorry, Councillor, what were you saying?

[   ] don't know why we have to use it.

We've been through this, Geoff. It avoids ambiguity later. Audit—

I'm sorry, but the whirring noise – my hearing aid.

Audit make their own recordings. Yeah, yeah, yeah, we know.

Exactly, Geoff. Miss Harding?

I was just saying – my hearing aid.

[   ]

So why don't we use theirs?

Perhaps if I were to sit where you are, Councillor, it wouldn't be so much of a problem.

That's not the point, Geoff. We can't use theirs because Audit—

[   ]

Councillor Grayford? Miles?

He's asleep again, Miss Harding. You'll have to come round this way.

My point is it could be an unnecessary dupe [   ]

Careful, Miss Harding—

Oh, I am sorry, Councillor.

I saw that coming.

It's all right, Miss Harding.

But your trousers—

It's only water, Miss Harding, it won't stain. Now, Geoff, you know as well as I do that – but really, I don't want to take up everybody's time going over it again.

You're not wasting Grayford's time. He's fast asleep.

[   ]

Is that better, Miss Harding?

[   ]

Wait a moment, I can't hear – now say something.

Right. You know why we're here today.

Sorry?

Why we're here today.

Yes, that's much better.

So, if I might begin by saying – is Grayford really asleep?

Like a baby.

Miss Harding, if you could—

Miles! Miles!

What? What? I was awake.

Good. So if we can get down to business—

Finally.

Please, Geoff. Now, the death of Councillor Goss—

The tragic death.

Thank you, Miss Harding. The tragic death of Councillor Goss has implications for the council as a whole, quite apart from the immediate problem that an important road was blocked for most of this morning. The loss of revenue from that alone has implications.

Excuse me, for one road? For one morning? How much traffic do we usually have on that stretch?

T and E haven't given me exact figures yet, Geoff, but

it's estimated closing the road represents a revenue loss of between five and seven thousand pounds. That's before we include the cost of Councillor Goss's bodyguard—

We're still paying them after what they let happen?

Two of whom are dead, two required urgent, serious medical attention. We will of course be making the contracted payments to any dependants and covering such medical costs as arise.

But – perhaps I'm being naive here, John – but the person they were contracted to guard was killed. Doesn't that make them in breach of contract, or negligent? I mean, if they died protecting Councillor Goss and Councillor Goss was still alive, then fair enough make the payments, but – I don't want it to be said that we're rewarding failure.

I think that's a little harsh, Geoff.

I'm just trying to be realistic. Somebody here has to be. I think we need to take a good, hard look at whether making these payments is justified.

I've already done that, Geoff. Their contracts guarantee the payment if they die in the course of their agreed work. That's all.

So there's no performance element? No minimum standards? That's just typical.

It was a standard contract for personal security personnel drawn up ten years ago.

And it's never been reviewed? And don't we have people dying every week? We don't pay them bonuses.

We haven't had anybody dying in post since then.

What about Eastbourne?

Eastbourne isn't us. And those weren't personal security. Now, with all due respect, Geoff, these payments are a side issue—

I don't think they are. I mean, how much are we paying these, what are they, dependants?

Five thousand each.

And I suppose that's as well as a pension.

That's in lieu. The original contract gave them a choice.

Well that's something, I suppose. But it's still ten thousand pounds. Add that to the toll revenue—

Quite. But if I can go back to the issue of Councillor Goss—

All I can say is you're being very flippant about the loss of fifteen sixteen seventeen thousand pounds. That's three additional toll-booth operators for a year. For a year, John.

I'm not being flippant at all, Geoff. The whole thing is going to cost more than twenty-five thousand. I mean, what do you know about the accident?

Accident? I heard it was a shooting.

Well, the earliest reports indicate—

A shooting? Surely this is a sign—

Not signs again.

I know you're not a believer, Mr Plaice, but—

Oh, I'm a believer, Miss Harding, I believe it's all—

[ ]

Please, both of you. Shots were fired, but they don't appear to have been the cause—

[ ]

Grayford?

Did he just say something?

I think he's asleep again. Should I—

Leave him, Miss Harding.

But shouldn't he—

Let him sleep.

Now, Geoff. He may have something to contribute.

Doubt it.

Mr Plaice!

If I could remind you why we're here—

Yeah, Councillor Goss, tragic death, consequences.

Exactly. Now, as far as we can tell, it was an accident. The councillor's car was involved in a collision with a vehicle heading from the opposite direction.

His car? So the Bentley's a [   ]. I had my eye on that.

Mr Plaice, really!

It's another cost, Miss Harding. This is just getting better and better.

And it's going to get worse, Geoff. Now, the driver of the other car is believed to have been intoxicated. He had been seen earlier driving in an erratic fashion.

And nobody thought to do anything about it.

A report had been filed.

So that's all right then. We have a report. Nice to see T and E still have priorities.

Now, Geoff.

So where did these stories about shooting come from?

The shooting seems to have been after the crash. One of the bodyguards, he had been in the crash, appears to have become disoriented. He saw another vehicle heading towards them and thought they were under attack—

Typical.

He responded as he had been trained.

How terrible! Was anybody hurt?

I'm afraid so, Miss Harding.

And we're paying these clowns?

Actually we're paying their dependants.

Big difference. It's still costing us money.

I'm aware of that, Geoff.

But I seem to be the only one who cares.

I care, Mr Plaice.

Do you, Miss Harding? You're taking it very well. This seems to have been a complete [   ]

The Lord disposes, Mr Plaice.

And, as usual, makes a complete fist of it.

If we could focus on the matter at hand, Geoff—

I am focusing, John. That's why I'm so bloody furious.

Now, the bodyguard in question.

This other car – do we know what they were doing there?

So far, no. Though I have heard they were carrying council IDs.

So? Half the town—

The driver and passenger of this third car are both in hospital. We haven't yet been able to question them.

Convenient. And I suppose we're paying for that.

If they're council we're obliged to. And there's more. The third car, when it crashed, crashed into a house front – two house fronts, in fact – causing, apparently, considerable damage. We will almost certainly have to pay for that.

I don't see why.

But, Councillor, the damage is surely the result of the actions of one of our employees.

We don't know that, do we, Miss Harding? More importantly, can they, the householders, prove anything? Who are they anyway?

We don't yet have the full details. This is still a police matter, and they haven't yet completed their investigation.

Which is something else we'll have to pay for. This is getting better and better.

We can't avoid paying the police, Geoff.

I don't see why we're still using them.

You know perfectly well, Geoff. If we want access to London—

Yes, we have to give them the contract. But they're just a waste of money. All they do is make trouble when something like this happens.

Quite, Geoff, and the contract is an issue that will be addressed by the restructuring. Now, if we could please move on to the other implications, which are possibly more significant. I mean that one consequence of this is that there will have to be a by-election.

And how much will that cost us?

Obviously, campaigning costs will be met by the various candidates.

Yes – but ballot papers, officials. These things cost.

There's no way round it, Geoff. We can't not have an election.

I don't see why not.

Because, Geoff, it would cost more not to have one.

I don't see why.

Because Labour will see this as a chance to pick up one more seat. They'll be pushing for this election, and they can make trouble for us if we want the restructuring to go through.

They can't win that seat! They've never won that seat!

They think they can. Councillor Goss was unpopular.

He promised a lot, sure, but that's just politics. What do these people want?

The councillor failed to manage expectations. It is possible we could pay a price for that.

All the more reason for us not to have an election.

That could result in some disturbances.

So? Let T and E deal with it. Or Parks and Libraries.

Which would mean overtime.

Overtime sure, but—

Geoff, we have to have this election. The costs to us, political and financial, would be worse if we didn't. Without Councillor Goss our majority falls to one seat. There are two independents. They are now much more important. If we want this restructuring to go through we need to marginalise them again, and we can only do that if we get a Conservative back in Councillor Goss's ward. Once we have the two-seat edge we'll have more leverage with the independents, and then it will be back to business as usual.

OK, but—

But we have to have this election, and we have to win it. Labour are going to put up a strong challenge. Now, Goss made himself so unpopular they might even pick up some votes. We also have another factor. It's likely Frank Henderson will put himself forward again.

He doesn't have a prayer. Not in that ward.

The danger isn't that he'll win. Miss Harding?

Can't we have him barred from standing? Doesn't he have a criminal record?

The criminal record route is one we'd rather not go down.

But his is for violence! Mr Plaice's—

Thank you very much, Miss Harding.

I was just saying, Mr Plaice—

Of course you were.

Calm down, Geoff.

I am calm, John. And for your information, Miss Harding—

Sit down, Geoff. And no, Miss Harding, it's not possible.

A simple miscarriage of justice.

Quite, Geoff. Now, as I was saying, the danger is not that Henderson will win, it's that he'll attract enough of our vote to give Labour the victory.

But surely our voters wouldn't support a hooligan like Henderson?

Hooligan like Henderson? I like the sound of that.

Oh look, Grayford's awake.

I've been awake the whole time.

That's not what it looked like.

You're not the most perceptive of people, are you, Plaice?

Please, both of you. There are more important matters we—

OK then, I just wondered, since Grayford has been paying such close attention, what his ideas are on this.

Well, Plaice, since you asked, it seems to me that the answer is obvious. We go ahead with the election.

Yeah, and Henderson?

Look, there are two factors here. One, Goss was unpopular. Some things were promised and not delivered, and that business with the children didn't help.

The poor souls.

Quite, Miss Harding.

[   ] them right for playing so close to the road. I suppose we should be grateful they weren't from his ward. How much did that cost us?

Five hundred to the parents of each.

That's a lot of money, John.

It was based on expected future earnings.

From that ward? They're lucky we gave them anything. Future earnings my arse.

Whatever the reason, Plaice, there's a lot of resentment because of that, and the voters may want to punish us for it. Correct?

Yes, like you said, it's obvious.

Secondly, what is Henderson's big issue? Mr Plaice?

[   ]

That's right. The toll roads.

So?

So there it is. The answer's obvious.

You may need to give us a little more detail, Miles.

As you wish, John. This is what we do. Firstly, we don't cancel the election, but we do delay it. Until, say, the result of the police investigation. We should announce that we don't want to have the election under the shadow of these unanswered questions. That way, we can make anyone calling for an immediate election look, well, overeager. The observers will back us on that.

OK.

The police will be happy to drag the investigation out for a few months.

That'll cost us.

Which will give us some time for the resentment against Councillor Goss to die down. Are you with me so far, Plaice?

Go on.

In the meantime we do something to defuse the toll issue in that ward. What's the biggest complaint people have about the toll?

They have nothing but complaints. Ungrateful bastards.

Actually their most frequent complaint is about having to pay a toll to reach their place of work.

Exactly, John. And this is where T and E come in. We announce a modification to the existing one-way system. T and E can determine where the majority of motorists in that ward work, and devise a system that enables the majority to get to their places of work without going through a single toll.

[   ]

Thank you, Miss Harding.

OK, OK, don't go overboard. Assuming T and E can do this, how can they do it without making it look like obvious electioneering? It could backfire.

Obviously we don't tell the public why we're doing it. We announce the new routes, there'll be the usual grumbles, and then they'll start noticing the loophole. We let them think they've outwitted us, then campaign on making no more changes while we're in office. This will be a couple of months down the line. By then Councillor Goss will be a fading memory and Henderson will have nothing to campaign on, our voters will remember where their loyalties lie and vote for us. A month later we reintroduce the tolls.

That might cause some resentment, Miles.

Only in the short term, John. We'll run some scare stories

about falling revenues to prepare the way. There'll be some complaints but in the end they'll accept it.

It's certainly a promising course of action. Geoff?

In the meantime we lose an awful lot of revenue. Are Finance going to allow that? Are Audit?

I suggest we keep Finance out of this altogether. I can take care of that aspect.

Family connection, Grayford?

Geoff, please.

I know, John. But has he even considered how much this is going to cost?

Probably in the region of forty-five thousand.

[ ]

I think it's a price worth paying. And it's not all bad news, Plaice. The loss of revenue may even give us a reason to introduce the education reforms you've been banging on about.

Nursery education has been a drain since it was introduced.

See, Geoff? You stand to get something out of this as well.

It's an open-ended commitment. Every year there's another lot of the little bastards. What do they need to read for anyway?

Quite, Geoff. I think we can leave that discussion to a later date. Is everybody agreed then? I'll talk to T and E.

I support Councillor Grayford on this.

Thank you, Miss Harding. Plaice?

I suppose it's [   ]

Unanimous, then? Good, unanimous.

At last. Does this mean we can switch this bloody thing [   ]

Margaret

When the tape ended Alan said: 'Shall we open another bottle?'

Margaret contemplated her half-empty glass. It was a dangerous time of night. She decided to let him decide. 'You still haven't said how you got it.'

'There's a bloke, Jim, in my department.' Alan was already on his feet, heading for the kitchen. 'He knows people at the harbour.'

'The tape.'

'It's been going round the office ...' What he said next was lost in the clink of glass as he fussed at the wine rack. She took another sip – no, a swig – from her glass. The bitter taste still came as a surprise. This batch wasn't as good as the last, but then the wine shipped out to England was supposed to be leftovers, the dregs the French wouldn't touch. She'd heard even the wine the French kept for themselves was falling in quality, though she wondered why this could be and how people could tell. What was the standard? Or did people have higher expectations now, which made them think the wine was getting worse?

Margaret believed in standards: of speech, of dress, of responsible behaviour. She believed in setting an example. To drink a bottle of wine each was irresponsible. But to stop now would feel like a waste of an evening …

She emptied her glass. 'So, do you think it's real?'

He came back with a bottle of the same wine. 'It sounds too elaborate for a hoax. The crash was barely a week ago. Who would have had the time? And we know the meetings are taped.'

'We could ask Denise.' Though she could imagine how that would go: Denise would tell them nothing – and be right to tell them nothing.

'This hasn't come from Audit.'

'But Audit would know if it was real.'

'They do sound like the real people,' Alan said carefully. 'The story is that they make these tapes for their own benefit.' He fiddled with the bottle opener, a little German device that folded away neatly but sometimes jammed. 'To keep themselves in line. So they can't deny they were in meetings, or pretend they opposed something they supported. It's insurance.'

Margaret knew this already. 'It's stupid.'

'It's a way of enforcing discipline.'

Alan said this as if it was the clinching argument. He approved of discipline, as did Margaret. Even so, it was stupid. She sighed heavily. 'It's stupid because we get to hear it. And if we can hear it, anybody could hear it. That could damage the council.' She felt a sensation that, without the half bottle of bad wine, she would have recognised as anger. The tape was the kind of thing that should not have been allowed to circulate – if it had been played to her by anyone other than Alan she would have filed a report. 'If someone like Louise hears this ...'

'I don't think it's likely to get out.' The cork finally came out of the new bottle. 'Besides, it doesn't really tell us anything new. We always knew the tolls were political.'

'*We* did.' She held out her glass. 'But to have it spelt out like that, so anybody can hear it. They could lose the election on that one alone. If they ever call it.'

'You heard them. They can't not call it.'

'If it's real.' Despite being from a bottle with the same label this wine was less astringent. The labels were a con, she thought. Everybody knew it and still felt cheated. 'And if they did cancel the election, would it be so bad?'

Alan laughed. 'So you're against democracy now?'

'Since when were you such an admirer?'

'It's worth thousands in grants.'

'Which we spend protecting the observers.'

'We are a modern, democratic state.' Alan's face assumed the abstracted expression it always did when he marshalled an argument. 'We have to hold elections. Do you have a better idea?'

'Yes.' Margaret felt a flush of warmth. 'Enlightened dictatorship. It's better than having trouble every five years. It's what Braddon's working towards anyway, isn't it? It would cause less disruption. Even by-elections are a nuisance.'

'I see.' Alan's tone suggested he was about to employ the dialectical method, the only remnant of his political science education. 'So you would disenfranchise people for their own good?'

'Exactly. Why are elections so important anyway?' Margaret didn't give him a chance to answer her question.

'It's not about differences in principle, is it? It's about patronage. If the Conservatives win, their supporters get jobs. If it's Labour, their supporters get them. All the fighting is about jobs. And why are there so few jobs? Because of the fighting.'

He put down the bottle and applauded. 'You should form a third party, Mags. Look, you have to work with the system you have, otherwise you're like the Helmstoners, hoping the end of the world will solve all your problems.'

'Elections just make things worse.' She felt relaxed, as if she was about to fall asleep; at the same time she felt lucid. The terrible clarity that comes with the second bottle of wine. 'People get hurt. Besides, there's already a third party.'

'People will get hurt anyway. That's the price of living in a modern, democratic society.'

'It's not a price worth paying.'

He shook his head, as if dismayed by her cheap rhetorical trick. 'You're getting soft, Mags. You're spending too much time with Louise. Is this where you tell me I haven't seen the things you've seen?'

Margaret yawned. 'No.' This was a disagreement they seemed to have every few weeks. But it was worth having again, if only because she was right and Alan was wrong. 'But if you had you wouldn't be so keen on the democratic process. You don't realise how sheltered you are.'

He sipped the wine and grimaced. 'I think I do. I have you constantly reminding me.'

'I have to remind you.' She forced a small laugh. 'Otherwise you wouldn't know how sheltered you are.'

'Oh yes, because I'm the favourite nephew of a councillor. I've had it easy.'

'You know that's not what I meant.' Her heart sank, a little. She hadn't expected him to resort to his uncle so early. 'I mean, you don't see anybody outside your immediate circle.'

He wasn't listening. 'You know, it annoys me when people throw that in my face. It's so easy. It saves them having to think of anything relevant.'

'I didn't mean that.' It would be so easy, she thought, to tell him, *It annoys me when you use your family as a way of avoiding every question.* But that would lead directly to a real argument. 'I meant you in your office, all of you, who don't actually see the public.'

'Unlike the heroic Welfare, I suppose.' Alan tried to sound light-hearted but she could sense the strain. 'T and E have plenty of contact with the public, thank you very much.'

'Oh, really.' Her laughter came out harder than intended. 'They might. You don't. Jack barely leaves his office and you never travel anywhere without an armed escort. And when you come home you come here, to another enclave. Do you remember what the last election was like?'

'Yes. Clearly.' He was frowning, not looking at her. She held out her empty glass. He filled it, still without looking at her, as if out of courtesy to the glass rather than her. 'Besides, this is only a by-election. *And* in one of the more civilised wards. It's not as if we're talking about the sort of places you work. Jack and Denise live there. We can't afford to. Practically every house has a satellite dish. That's how dangerous it's likely to be.'

'We could afford to live there.' She softened her tone. 'But I still think there will be trouble. Whoever circulated that tape – that's *supposed* to cause trouble.'

'There's always going to be a certain amount of trouble.' He refilled his own glass. 'I think this bottle's better than the last one.'

'That's because it's not very good wine. When it's good wine, it's the first bottle that tastes better.'

'Magsy's second law of viticulture.'

They fell silent. Margaret studied the wine in her glass. It did taste better than the last bottle. The inconsistency annoyed her. She asked: 'Should we have Tim and Louise over for dinner this Friday?' Their usual discussion. It would end with them inviting everybody and then accepting whoever came.

'I like Tim.' Alan drifted back from his own thoughts. 'He's responsible.'

'Despite being married to Louise.'

'Is she really that bad?'

'I've seen her with clients. She treats them like … like …' She struggled for the analogy.

Alan shrugged. 'I don't think she's so bad.'

'Oh, for a dinner she's fine. But you haven't seen her at work.'

He grinned. 'So, out of all our friends, who has the most clout? I think it's you and Louise.'

'Rubbish. What about Jack? He is your boss.'

'No, no.' He waved the arm not holding the wine glass. 'You've got more clout than any of us, you two. Yes, I do what Jack tells me to do. But Jack does what the committee tell him. We're both cogs in the machine.'

'Denise has authority. And Kieran.'

'I think you're wrong.' Alan seemed to believe that people wouldn't mind when he told them they were wrong. 'As a department Audit has power,' he explained, as if he really thought it was something she wouldn't know. 'But as far as decisions go Denise is in the same boat as the rest of us. And Parks might have issues around discipline, but Kieran still has to follow orders. Do you really think he's a Henderson supporter?'

'I'd be surprised. He's not ...' This time she found the word: 'Political.'

'That's where Henderson gets his support. You'd be surprised, the people you think are intelligent who turn out to support him. Kieran's just the type to say, "Well, he does have a point." He's too good-natured for his own good.'

Margaret pounced. 'So you think people support Henderson because they're too nice?'

'Some of them. Or they think they're better than those of us actually trying to improve things. I mean, what do you know about Siobhan's politics?'

'She thinks she's above that kind of tittle-tattle.' Margaret thought about the planned dinner: Tim, as usual, would not say very much. Louise would talk enough for two. Should they have more people? Someone who could talk as much as Louise? 'Tell you what, we'll invite them to dinner as well. You can ask Kieran then.'

'Even if he told me he wasn't. Especially if he told me he wasn't ...' Alan stared into the middle distance. 'I don't like Kieran. Am I allowed to say that?'

'As long as nobody else is listening.' Margaret smiled. 'I don't like Siobhan,' she said, more loudly. 'Why don't you like Kieran?'

'Because he's too ingratiating. Do you know what he reminds me of? Do you remember Paul Gurney's dog?'

She did: the huge, black mongrel a neighbour had

bought from a farmer after the house opposite had been burgled. A ferocious-looking beast with heavy paws and peculiarly mismatched teeth, the dog proved to be comically nervous. It hid behind chairs when strangers entered the room, and was wary of children and the neighbourhood cats. The dog was a joke until Paul Gurney had taken it for a walk on the Level.

Margaret laughed, though it was a story that ended badly. 'Do you think he'll turn?'

'Kieran? I don't think there's anything there to turn. If Kieran were up to something Siobhan would tell us. Eventually.'

'I doubt it.' Margaret tried to remember the last time Siobhan had told them anything worth hearing. 'Siobhan's useless, in that respect.'

'Or loyal. Which means he's up to something.' He paused, as if suddenly unsure of what he'd said. He shook his head, as if to dislodge a troubling thought. 'Do you know who Siobhan reminds me of?'

'Paul Gurney?'

He giggled. 'I was going to say Tim.'

'You mean she's dull.'

'No duller than Tim. But Tim gets away with not gossiping because he's a man. We're allowed not to talk.'

'You talk enough.' Margaret began to relax again. Even the tape had become unimportant. 'Maybe it's an Amex thing, the corporate culture. You know, maybe she should have married him instead of Kieran.'

Alan was still laughing. 'They haven't got a thing in common.'

'Apart from their jobs and personalities. Mind you, that would leave Kieran with Louise, and can you imagine what that would be like? Fighting to get a word in edgeways. Jack and Denise are happier.'

And then they talked about whether Jack and Denise were, despite appearances, happy; about how Tim might be happy and how Louise tried too hard to be amusing; they agreed Doug and Sarah were the only happy couple they knew. They talked until they had finished the second bottle, and then Margaret stumbled to her bedroom and lay on her bed and listened as Alan stumbled towards his.

Incident report #7841

This is a preliminary report pending additional statements from witnesses not yet questioned.

The accident occurred when Councillor Goss's Bentley was involved in a head-on collision with a Fiat 126 registered to Anthony Durlage. Anthony Durlage was subsequently questioned and provided evidence that the vehicle had been reported stolen two days earlier. The driver at the time of the accident has not yet been identified, but was a white male between the ages of 15 and 33. He was killed on impact, as were both Councillor Goss and his driver, John Tyrone.

It is not clear how the councillor's vehicle had become separated from his motorcycle escort, or how the escort came to lose formation. It has been suggested that they were engaged in a race along a stretch of road that has gained a reputation as a site for so-called 'toll-gate burning'. This has been denied by both surviving escorts. Their testimony is, however, confused and, in some details, contradictory. The transport officers on the last toll gate have confirmed that all the vehicles accelerated noticeably once they had passed the barrier, but that this acceleration was not out of the ordinary. They believe the Fiat 126 involved in the accident had passed through their gate several minutes before the motorcade and had similarly accelerated.

Whatever the reason for the loss of formation, there can be no doubt that this loss was a major determinant of the eventual collision.

It has been suggested that the collision was a deliberate act carried out for either personal or political motives. While the councillor was a controversial figure, without knowing the identity of the other driver this line of inquiry is purely speculative. The posters that have appeared claiming the act was carried out in response to the so-called 'Rose Hill massacre' have been traced to a single individual, now in the custody of Parks and Libraries. While we do not rule out the possibility that the collision was the result of a deliberate act on the part of the other driver, we would emphasise that there is at present no evidence to support this claim.

What is beyond dispute is that the councillor's vehicle was approximately 30–40 yards ahead of the escort when it was involved in the head-on collision. Our investigators have established that at the moment of impact both vehicles were travelling at approximately 45 mph, and both appear to have been driving in the middle of the road rather than the designated lanes. Both drivers seem to have attempted to turn immediately before impact. Goss's driver, John Tyrone, turned to his right. The driver of the Fiat 126 turned to his left. Councillor Goss and the driver of the other vehicle were either killed or rendered unconscious by the initial impact. John Tyrone attempted to climb out of the vehicle and was struck by the motorcycle ridden by Dennis Hastett. John Tyrone was killed instantly. Dennis Hastett was thrown over the crashed vehicles and died as a result of injuries sustained.

It has also been suggested the crash resulted from a game of 'chicken'. This suggestion has gained an unfortunate currency due to a) the frequency of accidents arising from this game that have occurred along this stretch of road, and b) John Tyrone's own police record, including the juvenile offences committed when he was allegedly known as 'Chicken King' (we are currently investigating the circumstances surrounding the release of these records). Finally, there are the circumstances of the crash itself. However, as we have been unable to obtain direct evidence from any of the occupants of the cars involved, we are obliged to discount this suggestion.

Thomas Lay was killed when he swerved to avoid the collision and was struck by the motorcycle ridden by Richard Peel. Peel himself sustained multiple injuries to both legs and lost consciousness for several minutes. His testimony as to the sequence of events is patchy and inconsistent. We have been advised that head injuries sustained during the accident that were not at first noticed by the medical team in attendance mean that his reliability as a witness is open to question. We are aware that copies of his initial statement have been circulated (we are currently investigating the circumstances of its unauthorised release). We would stress that some of the most sensational claims ('multiple shooters', the presence of other vehicles at the scene) have been denied in subsequent statements. It is true that some have also been reaffirmed. Our position at the moment is that none of Mr Peel's statements is to be regarded as authoritative.

Dougal Feeth, the fourth rider, also swerved to avoid the crash and was thrown from his motorcycle when he came into contact with a lamppost. Mr Feeth sustained bruising and concussion but was otherwise unharmed. He states that he believed the collision to be the result of a direct attack; hence, when he saw a second vehicle approaching from the same direction as the first, he opened fire with his council-issue sidearm. He now understands that this belief was mistaken and regrets any harm that resulted from his action. It is worth noting that Mr Feeth denies a) that Councillor Goss was engaged in any sort of race, and b) that he was playing 'chicken'.

The driver of the second car, Alexander Barrow, claims to have no political affiliations. There is no evidence to link him in any way with the Fiat 126. His claim that he was returning from a social occasion has withstood all investigation. While it is true he was 'out of his way' his claim that he used that stretch of road because it was 'usually quiet at that time of night' is not implausible.

He states that when he first heard the crash and saw the subsequent fire, his impulse was to stop to see if he could offer any assistance. He claimed that in the last five years he had seen two crashes on that road and had offered assistance on both occasions. His claim to have reported these incidents has since been vindicated. The press story that appeared denying this was based on prematurely released information. We are currently investigating the circumstances of this premature release.

Mr Barrow states that he saw someone running towards him from the side of the road. Mr Barrow states that he requested his wife to wind down her window to hear what the man was saying. It was then that he realised the man was holding a gun and seemed to be about to open fire on them. He states that he did not recognise the man as a council official because the man was not in standard uniform, and insists that he did not accelerate again until the first shot had been fired. Mr Feeth has claimed that the car pulled away when he ordered them to stop, and it was then that he opened fire. Bullets recovered from a house front at the site of the collision do not seem to support this claim. Mr Feeth admits to firing three subsequent shots: one, which missed, and another, which entered through the rear window of the car and struck Mr Barrow on his right shoulder. This caused him to lose control of the vehicle and crash into the house fronts of Nos. 52 and 54, causing considerable structural damage. The third shot was fired when Mrs Barrow, unhurt except for cuts from broken glass and severe whiplash, fell from the vehicle and, according to Mr Barrow, himself trapped in the vehicle, tried to run away. Mr Feeth stated that at the time he believed Mrs Barrow to be running towards him in a threatening manner. He has since conceded that he might have been mistaken. Mrs Barrow was struck in the lower back, sustaining considerable internal damage. Mr Barrow states that Mr Feeth then approached his vehicle. He reports that he was apprehensive as to Mr Feeth's intentions, and believed Mr Feeth might attempt to shoot him as well. The arrival of a Transport and Environment patrol vehicle meant that no further action was taken. Mr Feeth's original contention that Mr Barrow had been part of an assassination attempt was unfortunately given more credence than it deserved; the consequent delay in receiving medical attention may have resulted in the death of Mrs Barrow and the health problems subsequently alleged by Mr Barrow.

It should be added that while the incident exposed certain shortcomings in the disciplinary standards of some of the council security staff, this cannot be taken as a reflection on the training they have received. The Southern Region

Police Authority has every confidence in the standard of their contracted training services.

Pending further information as to the identity of the driver of the Fiat 126, and in the absence of any evidence that it was a deliberate act, we would class this incident as an accident.

Siobhan

Siobhan woke with a start and reached out to Kieran's side of the bed. He wasn't there.

She breathed a long sigh of relief and let her arm rest on his pillow, luxuriating in the sense of space and the contrast between the coolness on that side of the bed and the snug warmth of her own. In her dream (a bad one, again) she had been tied in a sack and thrown into a river. It had been one of those dreams in which she was both spectator and participant: she had stood with the crowd at the river's edge and watched herself being forced into the sack, conscious of both the other spectators pressed against her and the dark and textureless cloth that constricted her movements. The people around her, she was sure, had been bored. She didn't blame them: the events had had the routine feel of the public executions of the war years. There had been no hope of reprieve, or escape. As a spectator, even she had been bored.

All her friends had been there. Doug, whom she hadn't seen in months, had tied the sack. Denise had either read the verdict or decreed the punishment, and Margaret, she was certain, had nodded approvingly. Every element in her dream (the parts she could still remember) had been derived a little too obviously from her life. The only puzzle was the absence of Kieran, but then he rarely figured in her dreams – unless he was everywhere but invisible, the way God was supposed to be, though she had stopped believing in God when she was nine, and hadn't seen anything since to make her reconsider. At university she'd read *The Golden Legend* and recognised too much of her own world – the wars, the arbitrary cruelties – behind the miracle stories and saintly intercessions. All that had changed since then were the certainties of faith. Back then, dreams were portents, messages from God; now, only Helmstoners believed in dreams. For everybody else they were, at best, taken as evidence of buried preoccupations, a sign of what you thought when you weren't thinking, daylight fears revealing themselves in emblematic, pointless dramas. Her unconscious mind, she reflected, was almost laughably pedestrian: she felt suffocated, it provided an image of literal suffocation.

Laughable, until she considered the material it had to work with.

She turned to the alarm clock. Twenty past six. The alarm was set for a quarter to seven. She still had a few minutes to herself – provided Kieran didn't come back. With luck he wouldn't be home until after she'd left. If she could then stay at work for a few hours extra … There was always work to be done: one of the reasons she was considered a valued member of the team was her willingness to work those extra, unpaid hours. If it was possible to stay at work until after he had left for *his* next shift … If he had one, that is; if it didn't turn out he'd taken leave without telling her, and she would walk in, lighthearted, to find him sitting in their living room with the lights off, smiling as if he'd caught her out. And then he'd say, 'Isn't this just like old times?' or, 'Thought we should spend some time together, love. You know, I could easily think you were deliberately avoiding me.' Which would lead to, 'You shouldn't work so hard, love. It's not as if you're doing anything important there.' Which quickly became, 'I don't see why you work at all. I make enough for both of us.' Which in turn led to, 'I don't know why you have to be so stubborn. If somebody gave me the chance to stop working I'd jump at it.' Yes, she'd think, you would. Only you'd still want your drinking sessions with the boys, your shooting ranges and night patrols. You'd still want a *life*. If I gave up, I'd have nothing. I might as well put on a veil and never leave the house ...

The best would be if he didn't come back at all.

That thought again. It was as if the less she said, the more eloquent her thoughts became. Eloquent and murderous. She surrendered to them the way she would to a daydream, imagining the things that could go wrong: an accidental shooting, his patrol encountering smugglers who didn't co-operate, a brawl with a squadron from T & E, a 'misunderstanding' with a Regular Army Unit (but he was ex-army, he'd probably be known and liked by them). Liked. She was baffled at how many people seemed to like him, from councillors down to Scoomers. He'd fooled them all, the way he'd once fooled her.

She was supposed to be a successful member of the managerial class, in the top twenty per cent, one of the last to graduate from her university. There were people who envied her; there were people at Amex who respected her judgement, who reported to her, and hesitated before asking questions in case she thought badly of them. She was a valued member of the team: it had said so on her last half-yearly appraisal. At work, she mattered. At home, she found herself crying at unguarded moments and was grateful if her husband wasn't there to see it – she was grateful for every minute he wasn't there. The fear of him, she told herself, was worse than his actual presence; when he was actually there, he wasn't *so* bad – it was just that he was bad enough.

He came into the bedroom just as the alarm clock sounded, as if he'd been standing outside, waiting for a signal. Siobhan sat up, pretending to be sleepier than she was. She rubbed her eyes, yawned. 'You've just got back?'

She hadn't heard him coming home. Kieran was a big man, but he moved around the house quietly. He'd say it was because he didn't want to wake her. She thought it was because he hoped to catch her out.

He was in his field uniform, washed-out khakis patched at the knees with green canvas. 'It's not meant to look smart,' he'd say, but that wasn't the point. The shabbiness was cultivated. Everything about him was deliberate. 'I got back half an hour ago.' He began to unstrap the shoulder pack he claimed was unnecessary. 'You'd have noticed if you'd been awake.'

Half an hour ago. He'd been there when she thought she was safe. She could picture him, standing in the hallway, breathing softly. She tried to sound cheerful – or not cheerful, as if she didn't care. 'Quiet night?'

'Could have been worse.'

'What happened?'

'Lots.' He dropped the pack to the floor. He always

let it fall, seeming to relish the sound as it hit the floor, a reminder how heavy it was, how tough he was for carrying it so casually. 'But you don't really care, do you, and I'm too tired to talk about it so we'll leave it.' He unfastened his belt. 'I'm having a shower, then bed.'

Siobhan watched as he took off his jacket. There was no sign of mud or dirt, but then there rarely was these days, when he stayed in his jeep or his barracks, surrounded by his 'boys'. She watched the flex of muscle at his shoulder, the beginning of the pale scar that stretched across his back. She said, 'You should give up the night work.' She didn't know why she said it. She preferred the nights when he was away. Why was she pretending she didn't?

'Don't be daft.' He grinned at her. There was no friendliness in the expression: he grinned as if he was exercising the muscles in his lower face. He half turned in her direction and held his body still, as if posing for a photograph. He was a man who liked taking off his shirt in company, confident in his muscles and scars. 'You know I can't. It pays too well.'

She couldn't look at him without thinking of the days in the gymnasium, the weights lifted, the sparring, the hours spent in field manoeuvres and drill and, before that, the war. She imagined him working at his body with the same satisfaction other men derived from maintaining a car or a garden. Automatically she said, 'The money isn't important.'

'Then why don't you give up *your* job?' He turned away again, gazing out through the net curtains. He was now in profile, which emphasised his crooked nose, broken while sparring, or in a fall, or in actual combat – he changed his story carelessly, as if his past depended on his current mood. 'Besides, in my job, love, it's not as if I have a choice.'

'You could transfer.'

'You work nights as well, I notice.' He faced her with the same mirthless grin. 'Anyway, I don't want to talk about it.'

'No.' She swung her legs out of the bed. 'Go and have your shower.'

'I will.' He crossed the room and sat beside her. He smelt of petrol and sweat. When he leaned closer his breath was sweet. Whisky. 'While I'm here.' He laid a heavy hand on her thigh and began to nuzzle the side of her head. 'You've got the time.'

He wasn't drunk, not exactly. She could imagine the bottle passed round at the end of a fourteen-hour shift, the harsh jokes and weary post-mortems. For him, this was the end of a long day.

'No.' She lifted his hand away, tried to stand. 'I haven't.' Sometimes, if he was very tired, this worked.

He pulled her back on to the bed. 'Course you have.' In a quick move he was kneeling over her. 'This won't take long.'

She laughed. Sometimes appealing to his sense of the ridiculous could make him stop. 'You're such a charmer.'

This time he didn't laugh. 'I know. Aren't I?' He pinned her wrists above her head, holding them in place with one hand, reaching down to the waistband of her knickers with the other. His face had the intent expression of someone performing a routine mechanical task while thinking about something else entirely. This, she imagined, was how he looked when he assembled a rifle. She was reminded of her dream. Doug had tied the sack with the same expression.

'Listen,' he said, as if about to explain something. He pulled at the elastic of her waistband, pulling the knickers down her legs. Still she tried to make a joke, to speak as if what was happening wasn't happening, or was normal.

'It's a good job that's not my favourite pair—'

'Listen to me.' He put his free hand over her mouth and frowned slightly. 'I'm tired, I don't want to hear you talk.' He wasn't looking at her face, but at his hand, the one holding down her arms. 'I said this won't take long.'

He took his hand away from her mouth and used it to pull down his underpants. He pushed her knees apart with his knees, then all she saw was his collarbone and the veins in his neck. She closed her eyes and tried to think of nothing.

It didn't take long. When he was finished, when the weight of his body was lifted, she breathed deeply and shuddered. Her jaw ached from how she had clenched her teeth.

He stood over her. He ruffled her hair and smiled absently. 'Thanks, love. Now for the shower.' He pivoted smartly for the bedroom door and almost stumbled on the underpants still around his ankles. For a split second she wished he would lose his balance altogether, pitch forward and crack his skull against the doorframe. She would have to call for an ambulance and, because he was Parks and Libraries, one would come, but it would be too late.

It wasn't until she heard the sound of water falling that she was able to stop thinking about the accidental death of her husband – and looking forward to it. And what, she thought, as she picked herself up from the bed, did that say about her life?

And yet, minutes later, when Kieran returned from the bathroom, he smiled at her, as if nothing unusual had happened. 'Still here, then?' He sounded pleased with himself, as if her being there was down to his efforts, as if she had been sitting on the bed in some post-coital erotic reverie. Without saying anything she went to the bathroom. The floor was wet where he hadn't drawn the curtain, but at least he hadn't used the last of the hot water.

She wanted to be somewhere else.

The water turned cold after the first minute. She gritted her teeth and stayed under. She could grow used to the cold water, if only for the sense of relief when it stopped. She could almost believe the chill meant she was cleaner, that what had just happened had not happened, and that her life was like everybody else's: like Denise's, or Louise's, or Sarah's.

For a moment, she felt close to tears. Then, abruptly, there was no question of crying. It was easy, she thought, like suppressing a sneeze. There was even some satisfaction: she could control her emotions, or their outward signs, which came to the same thing. She turned off the water, and shivered as the warmth returned to her body.

She stepped out of the bathroom wrapped in the towels he had left damp. She tiptoed into the bedroom where he lay on the bed. She didn't look at him in case he was still awake and wanted to talk. He seemed to be asleep, but she knew he was a light sleeper. He could be woken by the faintest rustle of clothing, by the creak of a floorboard in the kitchen, by somebody looking at him. She pulled on her clothes under the towel, shivering. His revolver, in its holster, was attached to the belt looped over the back of the chair. She tried not to look at it. She knew she wouldn't be able to pull the trigger; even if she could, she'd miss.

She left her bedroom, buttoning her blouse. This was not how other people lived.

She was in the kitchen, spooning instant coffee into a tin mug, when she started to cry, quietly. From behind it might have looked as if she was laughing. She stood by the kitchen table he'd taken from a smuggler's house, her shoulders shaking.

This was not how other people lived. It's time I did something, she thought, as she always did. But her mind went no further than that, held back, she thought, like a dog tied to a post, a weather-beaten mutt with the bark kicked out of it, circling a back yard or some Scoomer allotment. She kept coming back to her own weakness. What could she do against someone like Kieran? He had too many connections: the people who worked for him, the ones who owed him favours, allies all over town. Who did she have? Tim, Louise's husband, the only one of her friends not to work for the council, a placid, dry man who seemed not to notice or care how his wife flirted with their friends. If he couldn't see something as obvious as that ...

But that was why she liked him: *because* he didn't see.

She dreamed of leaving. Dreamed, not thought, because to think would have involved making plans. At Amex they occasionally heard of jobs in other countries: the States, the Far East. She should apply for one of those. She wouldn't tell Kieran. She wouldn't even bother packing a suitcase. The first Kieran would know would be when she didn't come home that evening. At first he'd think it was overtime, and not care. Then, as the hours passed, he'd grow angry with her, then concerned – not concerned for her, but about her, because she was his property. He'd call her office, to be told: 'She left this morning ... Didn't you know?' She could imagine him throwing the phone across the room, kicking over chairs, breaking whatever came to hand. She would be in Berlin, or on her way to Seoul, where he couldn't reach her.

It was another dream.

By now, most of our readers will have heard about the recording, purportedly of a clandestine meeting of some of our elected officials. A happy few have even heard the recording itself. Your columnist is among this happy few, and found it very amusing – the talented young man who impersonates our favourite councillor catches exactly that characteristic tone of suave corruption. The rest of the cast is equally talented. The young lady pretending to be our dear Miss Harding sounds uncannily like that patroness of some of our town's crazier sectarians. Your columnist, ever the critic, feels, however, that she was given too few lines. Where were the tearful appeals to duty, or the random Biblical quotations that characterise so many of that lady's public statements? In this performance she is made almost likeable.

The alert reader will have noted that your columnist does not believe the tape is a genuine record. Amusing, yes, and perhaps possessing the deeper truth of art, but not an actual record of an actual meeting. Mr Grayford is not so unambiguous; Miss Harding is not so nicely ineffectual; Mr Plaice has been known not to swear; and nobody really knows what Mr Braddon is like. Yes, the tape is false, but your columnist believes it contains an essential truth. Sources within the council admit that Transport and Environment are indeed redesigning the system of toll roads, and, it is hinted, the redesign may indeed favour the late, unlamented Councillor Goss's old ward. Accident or design? Is this a case of life imitating art, or of satire as accurate reportage? There is no doubt plots are being laid, and Councillor Grayford has certainly shown no obvious sign of bereavement since the untimely end of his old rival. Your columnist does not pretend to know what will happen next, and can only observe that we continue to live in interesting times.

And, speaking of Councillor Grayford, it has come to your columnist's attention that that gentleman's favourite nephew has been seen drinking heavily in one of our town's more exclusive clubs. The young man – no longer so young, it must be said – arrived at the Beachfront with his usual crowd of bodyguards and sycophants at around eight o'clock last Wednesday evening. He then, your columnist hears, proceeded to drink his way through every bottle of spirits in the establishment, an endeavour which took him into the small hours – which leads to the reflection that either the not-so-young man is starting to slow down or the Beachfront now has a properly stocked bar. It is hard to know, dear readers, which is more unlikely. What provoked this spree? The rumour is that the not-so-young man had fancied himself the successor to the late Councillor Goss, a dream crushed when Uncle reminded him that councillors are appointed by the popular vote, and that, even supported by his uncle's formidable machine, that was something he could never win. The not-so-young man claimed he had changed – and promptly went on a bender, marked, it is said, by the kind of intemperate language he must have learned from Councillor Plaice. He was, it is said, once again prevented from causing a disturbance only by the swift intervention of his friends, a kindness he did not seem to appreciate. Once pulled from the fray, the ungrateful pup insisted on driving himself home despite being barely able to walk without assistance. It is to be hoped that he was not involved in the kind of incident that darkened the reputation of his uncle's late colleague – in so far as the late councillor had a reputation that could be darkened. Your columnist cannot remember the death of a public figure seeming more appropriate, or less lamented. Even members of his own faction see his death less as a loss than as an opportunity.

On an unrelated note: we are approaching the second anniversary of the 'planning permission applied for' notices in St James Street. Can any of our readers remember what was planned?

Finally, the editors have asked me to warn our readers that next week's issue may, once again, be published on Thursday rather than Tuesday. The fault, dear readers, is the usual one of shortage of paper.

Bystander

Louise

Whenever she had the chance Louise worked at home. She believed she worked better in her kitchen than in any of the small, usually overcrowded offices she shared with the rest of Welfare. There were fewer distractions and her kitchen table was larger than any of the council desks. She could spread out her paperwork without fear of its being disturbed, read her case notes, and type reports without the usual hysterical interruptions from her colleagues. On a good day the power supply was at least as reliable as in any council building. With her washing machine – it still worked – clanking in the corner and the smell of baking bread filling the room, Louise felt she could work *properly*.

She had been reading a case file when Alan called. A family (another one!) was refusing to send their child to a council nursery. The mother claimed religious reasons, the only ones recognised by the council. The case turned on whether the mother was a true believer or had simply invoked the Mission in her appeal because she thought it would help her case. From the paperwork in the file it wasn't clear. Louise had to read between the lines – which meant reading all of the lines. She had read barely half of them when Alan arrived.

His interruption hadn't been welcome, but he was a friend, so what could she do? He'd been working away from the office, he said, and had dropped by to ask if she and Tim wanted to come to dinner on Friday.

The invitation hadn't been a surprise. Out of all of their friends, Alan and Margaret gave the most dinners. They liked gathering people together. ('Of course they do,' Tim had once said. 'It's so they can keep an eye on us.') Louise, who enjoyed finding and preparing food, hosted at least one a month. Siobhan had given dinners in the past, but seemed increasingly awkward at dealing with more than two guests at a time. Denise could also cook, in her methodical way, but worked too many hours, and if you were honest the prospect of having her and Jack as hosts wasn't appealing, quite apart from having to walk back from their ward, which was simply unthinkable, or risk driving at night, which meant you couldn't drink – which would make an evening in their company an even grimmer prospect. So, if there was a dinner, it would usually be at Alan and Margaret's, where the food would be passable, Alan would tell them about the latest French wine he'd acquired, which was never much better or much worse than his last batch, and, towards the end of the evening, Margaret would start talking about responsibility and mean every word. Yet it would be a tolerable occasion: there would come a point when they would talk about whoever wasn't there, and then you could relax. Talking about your friends was safer than talking about work or the latest rumours about the Goss incident. When Alan or Margaret invited you, you knew what to expect, and complaining was worse than futile: it was beside the point. You went, you were appropriately grateful, and you joked about it afterwards. And a week or two later you went again.

Louise said of course they would come, as long as Tim wasn't working. 'You should come even if he is,' Alan had said. 'Margaret will be pleased to see you.'

And then, instead of going, he'd sat down, still with his black Transport jacket over his best grey suit, and given every sign of wanting to talk; and as, even more than most men, Alan usually talked about himself, Louise had decided to head him off by talking about Tim. 'I'm starting to think he's up to something …

'I first noticed last week,' she said. 'We were supposed to be having Doug and Sarah round, and then he phoned to say he might not be able to make it. Another meeting to do with their reorganisation.'

'Tell me about it. All *we* seem to do is reorganise—'

She wasn't going to let him start. 'So I thought nothing of it at first. Then I thought if he couldn't be there I might as well have someone else over. And I haven't seen Kieran and Siobhan out together for a while.'

'That might not have been a good idea. Kieran's Parks, Doug's T and E. They don't get on. There was a case recently—'

'I know about that interdepartmental stuff.' She cut him off quickly. 'I don't think Kieran takes it personally.'

'But Doug—'

'He's really not as bad as people think. Anyway, I phoned them and Kieran answered. He said he'd love to come but he was working and Siobhan wasn't home yet but she'd be back in an hour or so ...' Louise relished the details. She could have told the whole story in a sentence – or not told it at all, as it wasn't really a story – but where was the fun in that? 'Anyway, I tried again an hour later – the phones were actually still working. Kieran answered again. Siobhan still wasn't back and he wasn't sure now when she would be. She often works late and doesn't tell him. Poor old Kieran sounded quite concerned. I told him it was probably that phase two stuff Tim goes on about. He'd never heard of it. It's as if Siobhan doesn't tell him anything.'

'Their reorganisation.' Alan nodded. He was listening carefully, but only for an opening. 'I know all about that. They're trying to take over the old stadium. We had—'

'Exactly. Anyway, so I'd made the food – just a stew, but I had some good lamb from this farm out in bandit country. Strange little place, run by a man with one eye and his two blind sisters. Tim thinks the old boy blinded them himself so they wouldn't run away. I think it's unlikely. When you drive up to their house they all come out carrying guns, which you'd think would be a risk especially if anyone there harboured a grudge. Anyway, there we are, Doug, Sarah, me, and it's all OK, it's all perfectly normal, and we wait to see if Tim will get home before we start. And then it's eight o'clock, and half past, and there's still no sign of Tim, so we start eating. Anyway, Doug and Sarah stay until about half ten, and then they have to go. Sarah says it's because Doug's sister is babysitting and she doesn't really trust her. She means well, but she's a real Russell Street girl, you know, has never seen a telephone before and doesn't know how to use one. And as soon as they've gone Tim finally turns up. It was as if he'd been waiting until they'd left. So I asked him how his day had been and he said, "How much do you want to know?" In that tone as if it was all too dull to talk about.'

'It probably is. In our department—'

'I know. But Tim's not one to fight shy of being dull. You know him. He probably thinks his work isn't dull enough. *Hm, I don't like it. These figures are just too interesting.* Anyway, he asks how the meal went, and I told him how Kieran and Siobhan hadn't been able to come and he didn't say anything. And that's when I knew.'

'Knew what?'

'That he was hiding something.'

'Are you sure you're not reading too much into this?' Alan saw another chance. 'I mean, you don't think him and Siobhan—'

'Oh, I don't think it's that.' She waved away his objection. 'Whatever is going on, it isn't that. But you know Tim. He doesn't like discussing things. There was no discussion when we bought this house.'

'He had talked about moving here.'

'I'm sure he had – but not to me. He never mentioned it to me. I think he assumed I could read his mind. The first I heard that he was even looking in this area was when he told me he'd made the down payment. And then he was surprised I didn't already know.'

'But you didn't mind, did you, moving here?'

'No, but I didn't even know he was looking. I thought he wanted to move to Fiveways. The houses are bigger there.'

'It's a different culture. I lived there for a while—'

'Yes, it's a different culture – but it's *his* different culture. It's all Amex people out there. The gate people are

Amex security. They even have a special bus service. Do you know Tim and Siobhan are the only Amex employees who live in this ward? Literally the only ones. Everybody else is council – if they have a job. And if they haven't, then they're waiting for a council job. Tim and Siobhan are the only ones in Hanover who aren't.'

Alan said nothing, but only because the clank of the washing machine had risen to a loud whine. He adjusted his voice. 'But that's not so strange, is it? This town, you're either government or Amex or—'

'Or you're nothing. And there isn't much communication between them.' She grinned. 'Especially in this house.'

'I wonder if he's not ashamed of us.' Alan spoke as if expressing a long-held opinion. 'We're council. Maybe he thinks we're tainted.'

Tainted. Louise recognised the familiar signs of Alan's anxiety about who did and didn't like him. It was tiresome. Alan had the potential to be a tiresome man. Louise had discussed this with Tim; he'd said, 'It's more than potential.' She had to make it clear to Alan that she hadn't been talking about him. 'No, why would he think that? Tim likes his job. He just likes to keep it and his home life distinct. He never brings work home.' She waved her hand over the files on her table. 'Unlike me. That's why he didn't move to Fiveways. He'd be surrounded by work. He likes clear demarcations. And he makes decisions without asking first.'

Alan made a concerned face. 'That must be difficult for you.'

'Why should it be? I trust him. He usually makes the right decisions.' So far they'd led from a dark and peeling flat smack in the middle of Helmstoner territory – you were safe there, but, dear God, the endless vigils and praying, the dead-eyed raptures and rote fervency, the endless, toneless *singing* – to this house, with this kitchen and its lived-in, warm smells. Tim's decision had brought them to a snug existence in a safe area. He could easily have done worse. 'It's not as if he wanted to move to Russell Street, or even Lewes Road, with all the other pioneers. *That* would have been a questionable decision. No, Tim's secretive, but that's just something you get used to. And he's been like it since the beginning. My God, I'd known him for about three months when he first asked me out. Right up until that moment it was as if he hadn't noticed me. And I'm sure he would have preferred it if he could have asked me out already, to save him the trouble. He's like that. You'd think nothing was going on, then he presents you with a *fait accompli*. So I always think he's up to something. As a matter of course, I assume there's something going on.'

'Like what?'

'Moving to Fiveways? Joining the council? I don't know. How could I tell?'

Alan frowned, still unsure if she was joking. 'As far as I know he's not planning anything.'

'So he's getting worse.' She laughed. 'Now he's not even talking to his friends.'

'It could just mean he's not planning anything. He might be content.'

'I don't believe it. How could anybody—'

This time he interrupted: 'Are you content?'

'I don't know, Socrates. What does it mean, contentment? We live quite well. I like this house. We're pretty safe.'

Alan positively glowed with satisfaction. 'See? So it's better than it was.'

See? See what? What did he think they'd been talking about? 'It's different.'

'Right.' He drained his mug and placed it on the table with a flourish. 'Are you frightened of things getting worse?'

'Of course I am. Who wouldn't be? Although I think they are getting worse. Slowly. I mean, look at this place.'

'Your kitchen?'

'This town.' She sat back in her chair and sighed, as if this was something she was tired of explaining. 'The last ten years.'

Now he was surprised. 'You think it's getting worse?'

'Don't tell me you think it isn't.' But she already knew what he thought. Alan believed that things were getting better, and that the improvement was because of the council, and that the council was such a positive force mainly because he was working for it. 'My God, Alan, when you look at what your department has become.'

'We're safer than we were ten years ago.'

'Only because there's less to fight over. Look, Amex is the only corporation left. The central market is here only because Welfare underwrites the security costs. A third of the town is unemployed, and every other week another house burns down or blows up.'

'Gas mains. They—'

'And it's blamed on the gas mains. Everybody who doesn't work for us or Amex is in the black economy. When I started in Welfare there wasn't a single gate or barricade in the town. There wasn't a single roadblock, and I didn't need armed assistance every time I made house calls. Now look at the place.'

'But we don't have the' – he hesitated, as if for a difficult word – 'the anarchy.'

'Only because of the guns. Go anywhere south of Trafalgar Street, the old Laine. They still have the anarchy. People joke about Scoomers—'

'Nobody I know. The people from Moulsecoomb make a valuable contribution.'

'I wasn't saying you. But jokes are made, you can't deny that. And they're not made about those people. We don't talk about them. They're not even in the black economy. It's foraging. Subsistence. And there's nothing happening to make anything better. It's seven years since Welfare tried anything there, and Margaret can tell you how that ended. Nothing is being built. It's all rebuilt, or patched up. You know what it's like in the council's properties? Houses broken up, flats subdivided, whole families to a room? Well, it's worse there.'

'It's a rational approach to limited resources.' He stopped himself. 'I know that sounds like an official statement, but—'

'Do you know how many people leave every month? Fifty, sixty a month heading for London or Kent. Twenty a month turning up in the Dieppe camp.' She had papers in front of her: the files, the case histories of the families that couldn't or wouldn't stick to the rules; the families that didn't know there *were* rules … Her job was to decide what to do with them when they came back, or were brought back. While people like Alan (and her) lived behind gates, protected by armed patrols. *Life* was safer – for them. That didn't mean it was better. 'Some of them have been sent back five or six times, but they keep trying. And how much better is France?'

'I don't know. I've never been.' He frowned, as if she'd said so much that was wrong he didn't know where to begin. 'But I don't think you can say things are worse.'

'I thought you'd worked in France.' She softened her tone. If she wasn't careful they'd have a row, which might be fine at dinner over a bottle of wine, but not now, when she had work to do. And why was he still in her kitchen anyway? He had given his invitation. What else did he want? 'Doesn't your uncle have business over there?'

'I've never been.' He looked down at the table, then, seeing a file marked *Confidential*, averted his gaze. 'Really, I haven't.'

He suddenly looked so forlorn, so wrapped in self-pity, that she couldn't help turning the knife just a little. 'I know, I know, because you're the black sheep of the family. You're not like all the others.'

'But I'm not.' His voice came out low and harsh. 'The fact that I'm even talking to you proves I'm not. I may have got this job because of my family but at least I'm good at it. I actually try to earn my wages. Not like that idiot they've put in Finance.'

'There's a piece about him in *The Report*.'

Again, he showed surprise. 'You read that rag?'

'It's usually pretty accurate.'

'That's not the point. It's unlicensed.'

'Now you're sounding like your uncle.' She imitated: 'A threat to all the decent, hard-working people of this great town.'

'No.' He was suddenly angry. 'I know what I sound like, Lou, and it's not that. I'm fed up of people treating me like I'm some gilded son of privilege when it's just not true. I only see my uncle a few times a year. And, yes, I see Nathan occasionally, but it's not as if we're friends. And as for the rest of them ... So, no, I don't know about the business in France – they've never told me to go, and I haven't asked. And I won't ask. And even if they did tell me to go, well – I don't know. It would mean I'd be directly under their thumb. At least in the council I can pretend to be independent.'

He stopped, as if he realised he'd gone too far. They sat back in their chairs and didn't look at each other. Louise shuffled through some papers. Finally, Alan leaned forward. 'So, er, how was Sarah?' He sounded apologetic. He probably didn't want to leave on a bad note.

'She was fine.'

'Right. And Doug?'

'Surprisingly talkative.'

Alan offered a conciliatory smile. 'I'd like to have seen that.'

'You wouldn't have seen it. That's the point. Round you he feels – well, he realises he never had your education.'

'I've never talked down to him.'

'I don't mean just you. I mean all of you men. Our friends. Whenever you talk he feels self-conscious.'

'He said that?'

'Of course not. If he could say that then he wouldn't feel so self-conscious, would he? It's what he implies. Sarah sort of interprets for him. He doesn't have your education, so he makes up for it by emphasising the experiences he's had that you haven't.'

Alan nodded, as if she'd just given him the clue he needed to finally solve the puzzle. 'Hence all the stories about fighting. So he's not just trying to scare us.'

'He's doing that as well. It's his way of holding his ground.'

'I see. I really do. And that probably explains why he doesn't like Kieran.'

'Doesn't he?' Louise knew this was true but was surprised Alan had noticed. 'I don't know where you get that from.'

'You must have seen they never talk to each other.' Alan was enthusiastic again. Tim had once called him Alan the Explainer. There was something boyish about it, he'd claimed, the autodidact excitedly telling you the facts he'd learned earlier that day. Louise's own opinion was that Alan was becoming more like Jack: he was starting to take everything too seriously. For Louise, taking everything seriously was a sign of a failure of intelligence.

Denise had once said that Alan was a Monsieur Homais type. 'He's not telling you things because he wants to share knowledge. It's to demonstrate his superiority.' Denise's opinions – which Louise thought she didn't express often enough – usually had a ring of finality. You wanted to hear what she said about other people, and were nervous of what she might say about you.

'Or, to be fair, Doug won't talk to Kieran,' Alan rattled on. 'Every time they've been in the same room together Doug has made an excuse and walked out. Sometimes he hasn't even made an excuse. I thought it was the interdepartmental rivalry, as we're supposed to call it. But if it's personal as well …'

'Possibly …' She let him talk. At least he wasn't talking about himself.

'I'm sure of it. If Doug talks about the fights because he thinks we're a bunch of softies that's not going to work with Kieran. He's got the military background *and* the education. Doug can't compete with that. And it will get worse when Parks merges with T and E. Doug could easily find himself taking orders from Kieran. And when that happens Doug'll be on the next boat to France.'

'They've been talking about mergers for years.'

'This is going to happen.' Alan could hardly contain his satisfaction. 'Jack's on the sub-committee,' he added, as if this settled the argument.

'Really?' Louise hadn't heard there was a sub-committee. Presumably it was something Welfare wasn't supposed to know. 'What does Doug know about this?'

'He'd have heard the rumours.'

'Wouldn't Jack have told him what's going on?'

'It's interdicted.' Alan said it smugly, even by his standards. 'We can't discuss it with Doug.'

'That bad, eh?' Louise picked up a folder: she had work. It was time for another twist of the knife. 'Should I mention it to Sarah next time I see her?'

'That would be irresponsible.' Too late, Alan realised she was joking. 'You know what it's like, Lou. The council has its reasons.' Distancing himself from the council this time.

'Politics.'

'There's more to it than that.'

'Come on, Al. It's all politics in this town. In this country.'

'Maybe,' he conceded, then added, as if he couldn't help himself: 'But it's still better than it used to be. I'd rather have a deal in a council chamber than what we used to have.'

'You think? There's too much going on behind the scenes. Jack's committee, for one. If we didn't know Jack we'd never have heard of it. In Welfare we never know what's going on from week to week.' She took a deep breath; it was time to change the subject, otherwise he could be there all afternoon. 'And Tim's up to something.'

Alan was happy with the change. Possibly he thought he'd said too much. 'You could *ask* what he's planning.'

'Tim? You think I haven't? He just says "Nothing", and even the way he says it convinces me he's up to something. I know how he works. He'll come home one day, tomorrow or tonight, and everything will change.'

Alan laughed. 'Maybe he's having an affair.'

She laughed as well. 'If only he was that straightforward. If he can't tell *me* what he's thinking, how is he going to talk to another woman? He can't *start* an affair. He'd want to have started one already …'

The washing machine shuddered to a halt. Alan announced he had to get back to work, and reminded her, as if she was likely to forget, about the dinner on Friday.

Sub-committee for Resource Allocation Project (Non-participatory): interim report.

Susan DeMont (Audit); John Tenison (Transport and Environment); Nathan Grayford (Finance); Mike Brierly (Parks and Libraries).

This report is a follow-up to the preliminary report and incorporates some of the suggestions made by the steering committee. It has been issued to outline the current state of the reconstruction project, and to clarify the reasons for the delay in the production of the final report.

A number of issues highlighted in the preliminary report remain unresolved. Of these, possibly the most serious is the continuing unavailability of accurate financial reports regarding the departments as currently constituted. Mr Grayford assures the sub-committee that such information will be available in due course. The lack of current information means that financial forecasting with anything other than approximate accuracy is not possible.

Following the initial response to the preliminary report Mr Grayford undertook to supply alternative financial scenarios and budget projections. These have not yet been produced. Mr Grayford assures the sub-committee they will be produced within the next two, or three, weeks.

The sub-committee has met five times since the preliminary report was issued. All sub-committee members have attended each meeting with the exception of Mr Grayford, who telephoned in his contribution to the first meeting and was unavailable for the remaining four. Apart from the resultant lack of financial information, the sub-committee does not feel that this absence resulted in any serious loss to the work undertaken on structural issues.

The sub-committee would also like to take this opportunity to correct a factual error included in the preliminary report: the budget figures given for the last financial year (page 37, tables 9.4–9.8) actually relate to the financial year before that. Mr Grayford attributes this mistake to a misunderstanding within his department of his original instructions. The error is particularly significant in the case of Transport and Environment, which had undergone a considerable expansion/redevelopment in the period in question, possibly the most significant element of which was the wider introduction of the Supplementary Road-user Charge. Notwithstanding this drawback, the sub-committee feels it is able to make recommendations on the basis of provisional information. Our view is that the merging of Parks and Libraries with Transport and Environment will produce the following benefits.

1) Allow for standardised training procedures.

   As noted in the preliminary report, much of the training provided (small arms, automatic weapons, crowd control and public relations) is identical in both departments. Where there have been differences (field manoeuvres and light artillery for Parks and Libraries, urban tactics for Transport and Environment) these have on occasion led to a counterproductive rivalry and even friction (see Appendix B). If the departments are combined it will give the council the opportunity to 'reorganise' those units whose undoubted cohesiveness, while in some respects useful, has sometimes led them to act in a manner detrimental to official policy (see Appendix B).

2) Increase the pool of trained employees available for rapid deployment in a range of situations.

This follows on from 1. A larger number of trained personnel will enable the council to respond more effectively to situations as they arise. There have been occasions in the past where a lack of personnel in one or other of the departments has led to the perception of weakness, which has led in turn to some considerable disorder (see Appendix C for examples). A unified management structure will, in the long term, allow the council to assume control of all security functions.

3) Enable the council to maintain the current level of employment while simultaneously reducing on-costs.

The association in a single department of park management and library administration is a historical anomaly the sub-committee sees no point in continuing. While part of the library service (search-and-seizure, the tracking of unlicensed presses and broadcasts) is of obvious strategic importance and will remain within the newly formed department, the more centralised elements would more properly fall within the information and archiving remit of Audit. A more detailed list of the proposed changes is given in Appendix D.

Our proposed timetable for the reorganisation is given in Appendix E.

Siobhan

The third floor canteen in the main Amex building was quiet in the afternoons. The counter staff would have gone home, and the lights over the narrow counter would have been switched off. Sometimes Siobhan would find a small group practising their German or Japanese, but that day the only person there was Tim, who sat at a table by the window, writing. The only sound was the scratch of his pen on paper and the hum from the vending machine on the far wall, an old machine that offered tea and coffee and a hot chocolate drink nobody had ever tried twice. It was always on, even on the frequent days when it was empty; it was connected directly to the mains and could not be switched off, though it often broke down.

Tim didn't look up as she opened the door. There were papers spread neatly across his table, next to the calculator he carried everywhere. It was a coveted object, Japanese made and solar powered, one of only four or five in the whole building. Tim's was supposed to be a gift from visiting Germans as a mark of their gratitude for his liaison work, though Tim said they'd really given it to him out of pity. In Germany, they'd said, they were using mini-computers: tiny things that sat beside a desk and could perform thousands of calculations in seconds. The British operation was a poor cousin – you still had to book time on a machine the size of a house and the results, when they came, were printed so faintly they were sometimes unreadable. Tim had taken the Germans to the basement to see it. They'd been impressed at how the English managed to keep it working. When they came back up into daylight one of them had produced the calculator from a case and handed it to Tim. Here, he'd said, you can have this. We hardly use them these days ... Tim had carried it everywhere ever since, even taking it home with him at night. He was a careful man. He was, if anything, too careful: he sat in an empty room carefully, with a careful frown of concentration, making careful notes in what looked like an old school exercise book, no doubt carefully preserved.

She paused at the door. No, he hadn't noticed her. She walked over to his table. He still didn't look up. 'Tim. Sorry I'm late.'

It was as if she'd woken him from a light sleep. 'Siobhan.' He closed the book, but not before she'd had a chance to read: *We fear 'counterproductive rivalry' is an understatement ...* She didn't ask and he offered no explanation, leaving the book face down as he began to gather the other stray papers. 'I found something to do.'

'My meeting overran.' She dropped heavily into the chair facing him, without taking her bag from her shoulder or removing her jacket. 'It's the prep for phase two. Some departments still haven't given proper consideration to the implications.' Tim was collecting the papers with a kind of quiet urgency, as if these were documents she wasn't meant to see. She noticed he seemed to be gathering them in a particular order. This was typical of Tim. 'Do you want another coffee in that?'

'Thanks.' He gulped what was left and handed her the cup. It was a company joke that Amex was powered by coffee rather than electricity, though it was debated whether the hot brown liquid from the vending machine had ever had any connection with coffee. Siobhan thought it smelled and tasted like recently turned earth. A single cup could make her jittery; two, she was sure, would bring her close to hysteria.

By the time the vending machine had accepted her token and filled the cup Tim had cleared the table. He appeared calm. The coffee seemed to have no effect on him; nothing seemed to have any effect on him.

There were times when she wondered what *he* was hiding.

She nodded at his folders. 'You've been busy.'

'Still clearing up after phase one. The same problems you're seeing. Not all of it was thought through in as much detail as it could have been.'

Most of the people Siobhan worked with would have complained or appealed for sympathy. Tim sounded as if he was resigned to things going wrong. His tone suggested there would always be incompetence and bad decisions, but that it was the job of people like him to tidy up and make the best of what they found. Siobhan wasn't sure whether this was admirable or craven, though she appreciated his unflustered reserve. She had simple rules for conversation: talk about work, or the other people at work. She felt Tim was safe because he seemed to live by the same rules. She even looked forward to talking to him. Other people might think they were dull, but when they talked about procedures or exchanged rumours about management she felt normal.

'Our bid for the stadium will take some time yet,' Tim said, telling her something she already knew. 'We've lost nearly a year there.' He said it without regret, as if the year would have been lost anyway. The company would have given him something to fill the time; it hardly mattered what ... 'Liaison with the council isn't all it could be. Parks are dragging their feet. Or its feet.'

'Tell me about it. Phase two is supposed to start in two months.' She hooked her bag over the back of the chair and shuffled out of her jacket, her tone exactly that of tired junior management, confident and more amused than exasperated. 'And they're still arguing about the seating arrangements.'

'It'll be postponed.'

'That's what they always say.'

Conventional cynicism, exchanged like a password. 'Phase one was six months late,' Tim said, mildly. 'And phase two depends on having the additional land. We could find ourselves having to wait for the council to restructure first.'

Siobhan nodded, as if she had heard more than rumours. 'How soon is that likely to happen?'

'Before Parks and Transport merge? Six months. A year. I can't see us getting the stadium site before then.' He sipped the coffee cautiously. 'Unless there's a change of mind at Parks.'

'Unlikely. They're a stubborn lot.'

'Is that what Kieran says?'

The question caught her off guard. 'He doesn't ... he doesn't talk about his job.' It shouldn't have. It was an innocent question, even predictable. She thought she handled it well: 'You know him. It's as if they've taken a vow.'

'They're difficult. One week they'll be part of the council and waiting for a decision from cabinet, the next they're asserting their independence and telling us not to talk to them.' Tim didn't sound angry: for him the intransigence of Parks and Libraries was a fact of nature, like other people's incompetence. 'It's a shame Kieran isn't more ... tractable.'

'He won't help you.'

'Pity. It would be useful to have somebody on the inside. But these council types ...' He smiled. 'Have you ever felt like moving to the public sector?'

'Like everybody else we know?' She felt a sudden stab of panic. Was Tim thinking of leaving? And if he left who would she talk to? 'You're not, are you? I mean, I know the money's better, but there's no real security. Besides, you might end up working with Jack, or Alan.' She didn't add: or Kieran.

'Jack or Alan.' Tim was deadpan. 'Who do you think would be worse?'

'Jack.' He wasn't leaving. Siobhan felt herself begin to relax. 'Jack easily. He's a bit, I don't know, authoritarian.' This kind of conversation was a game she could play all afternoon.

'And you think Alan isn't?'

'He might be easier to work with. Some of the time.'

'He might be.' Tim gave one of his non-smiles, a tightening of the lips that was closer to a grimace. It was as if he'd just tasted the coffee. 'As long as you did exactly what he wanted.'

'So you think he'd be worse?'

'I think so. He's nice enough socially, but I don't trust him. And not just because of the way he sniffs around Louise.' Tim smiled at her surprise – a real smile this time, though it didn't last. 'Don't think I hadn't noticed. Louise doesn't think Alan's serious. She thinks he just wants to be liked by everybody. But you're right. The public sector is too risky. If Labour ever regains a majority Jack could be out of a job. And Alan definitely isn't safe.'

'Despite the councillor.' It was odd to think of her friends' jobs as precarious: they'd been with the council for as long as she'd known them. Yet all it would take would be an election, or, in Alan's case, something happening to his uncle. If a different car had crashed ... 'Poor Alan. That family connection he can never bring himself to talk about.'

'I'm sure it isn't easy for him.' Tim looked out of the window at the security gate and the concession stalls on the forecourt. There was a queue by the barber's stall. Amex men liked to be clean-shaven; it was a way of distinguishing themselves from council workers. 'You weren't here when the barriers went up, were you? Back then, Grayford was hated.'

'I was still in London.' She had a sudden, vivid memory of the flat she'd shared with three other ex-students. The last round of fighting had only just ended; the provisional government had been recognised. There was talk of rebuilding, full employment. She remembered it as an optimistic time, although disillusionment had taken only months. The flat had been a few yards from one of the first secure areas. She'd thought that would mean the area would be full of other aspiring young professionals, and, to begin with, it looked as if it was. But gradually the professionals had moved, either inside the gates or to another district. The flats around her started to fill – or perhaps they'd always been filled – with families that seemed to exist by scavenging. They collected rubbish from empty houses or furniture from occupied ones and bartered it for the food that trickled in from the suburbs. It seemed a miserable existence. She still thought about those families occasionally: by now they would surely have run out of things to scavenge. What had they done when there was no more furniture in their houses, after they'd traded the last pane of glass and length of pipe? The promised aid money might have helped: a soup kitchen here or there to keep them quiet, make-work in a state factory. That was all they'd get; and it might be enough. Now she lived in a different town, Siobhan could pity them: the same abstract pity she felt for the Russell Street crowds here. Back then she had thought the people around her were predators. They had stood in the corridors, or gathered on street corners or the decaying open spaces – men, women and children alike, whole family groups – as if they were watching and waiting. She started to think of herself as she was sure they saw her: as a potential victim. Then she'd met Kieran, just out of the army and working for one of the private security firms that controlled the City. He'd crashed a few times in their flat, a friend of the big brother of Steve, a frail maths graduate who wanted to go to America. Kieran had been charming then. For a little while, he'd made her feel safe. He had a friend, he said, who could get him a council job on the south coast, where it was quieter. There hadn't been any serious fighting down there in years ... When Steve heard that Amex were recruiting, and had an exaggerated respect for anyone who'd worked in London, she'd finally agreed to follow him down.

She lived behind the gates now. It didn't feel like much of an improvement.

She realised Tim was looking at her. 'Are you all right?'

'I was thinking of London.' She wondered if her expression had changed. 'We already had barriers there. When I read about them coming up here it didn't seem unusual.'

'I'd been here for about two years.' To her relief his attention went back to the security gate. But this was still an unusual conversation for him. Tim didn't usually talk about the past. Brooding on the old days, remembering the important dates, was for the poor and the religious. She wondered if Tim was leading up to something. 'It was a different town back then. The West Pier was still open. There was even some plan to rebuild the Palace Pier. I saw those gates go up. It was a waste of money. Nobody was going to attack Amex. We didn't have anything anyone wanted, except stationery and office furniture. I suppose they could have burnt it. And a mainframe that would be in a museum if this was a real country.'

'And dollar bills. They're legal tender in Suffolk.'

'So are chickens. It would have taken more than an angry mob to get into our vaults.'

'Management must have been cautious.'

'No. Caution didn't come into it. This was something they had to do. Grayford pushed through a regulation that any company employing more than two hundred people – us, in other words – were required to take adequate precautions. Which meant twelve-foot barriers. And have them built by an approved contractor. Which meant his brother-in-law.'

'Was it really that obvious?'

'It was actually his cousin. On his wife's side. But yes, it was that obvious.' He turned back to her. 'They were odd times. There was a lot of wild talk about what might happen. I was more worried about Louise. Welfare was different then. Back then, they didn't even have escorts.'

'Wasn't it standard procedure?'

'It is now. There were a couple of … incidents. But you can see why I was concerned. It was a high turnover job, even before the Trouble.' Siobhan nodded, though she was still confused by the terms people used. The Trouble was not the War, or the Wars, and was probably not the Russell Street Business that Jack sometimes referred to. There were names for each stage of the town's history and they changed depending on who was telling the story. 'There were some people,' Tim said, 'who think Welfare provoked the last incident deliberately.'

'The nursery school drive.' Siobhan had heard of this: the mad attempt to take every child in the town into council care. 'Louise told me.'

'She can joke about it now.'

'It must have been terrifying.'

'It was … grim.' He studied her expression with the bland curiosity of a dog then said, without any change of tone: 'I've applied for an overseas post.'

Her first thought was *You can't leave me*. She said: 'Where to?'

'Germany. Canada. The Japanese zone. I've applied for every one available.'

'That's quite a step.' And he'd get one of them, she was certain. Tim was exactly the person they needed. 'What does Louise think?'

'I, er, haven't told her yet.' Then, more firmly: 'You should apply as well.'

'I've only been here five years.' Which felt like a good excuse. Then she started as the canteen door was kicked open. It wasn't Kieran, but a security guard in full gear. 'Drill in ten,' he announced, the words muffled by his visor.

Tim nodded at him. 'Thanks, Ken.' When he had gone: 'I don't know who he thinks he is. Or what.'

'I can see why you don't sit with your back to the door.' She grabbed at the chance to change the subject. 'And these drills are just a waste of time.'

'Seriously,' Tim said. 'You should apply.'

'I don't know.' This was what she didn't want: to talk about herself or answer well-meant questions. 'I'm doing OK here.'

'What about Kieran?'

'I think he's happy with his work.'

'That's not what I meant.'

Her heart skipped a beat.

Tim sounded as bland as ever. 'There was one thing I've been meaning to ask about him.'

Her face felt hot. Her palms started to sweat. She tried to smile and sound bored. 'What about him?'

'Nothing special. I just wondered what he knew about that Goss business.'

'He says it was an accident.' She tried to say it as if it was something they'd discussed although she and Kieran never discussed anything. She didn't so much talk to him as eavesdrop on his monologues. 'I don't think he's had any direct involvement.'

'How good are his sources?'

'He says they're good.' *I have people everywhere. You can't do anything in this town without me hearing about it.* 'He says he has contacts.'

'Kieran.' Tim leaned towards her. 'He's a funny character.' But he didn't smile.

'He's …' There was nothing she could safely say about him. 'So when will you know? If you are leaving.'

'Six weeks. Two months.' Suddenly his hands were holding hers across the table, a light, reassuring pressure. Kieran couldn't hold her hands without reminding her how easily he could crush them. Tim's seemed no heavier than the fold of a blanket. 'You should apply as well. For your own sake.'

'I can't.' She blinked. She was suddenly close to tears. 'Kieran's job.'

'Then don't tell him. Go without him. Apply for the job. You'd get it. You have to get away. We'll help you.'

She clung to his hands. She felt dizzy, as if she was about to slump across the table. 'But—'

'You've as good a chance as anybody else. And you have to get away from Kieran. The man is trouble. Listen, this is something you have to do.'

She couldn't speak. She could only clutch his hands and stare at him, barely conscious of his soft, low voice repeating, as if to someone in shock, that this was something she had to do for her own good. It felt, for a moment, like a hallucination: she could see and hear him, but she didn't believe it was happening. How could Tim, of all people, know? Louise must have guessed and told him, that was the only possible explanation. But how did Louise guess? She held his hand until he grimaced and said: 'We'd better go down now. Drill.' She wiped her eyes. They went down to join the crowd in the forecourt.

To: N. Grayford

From: S. DeMont

Re: Financial information

As mentioned in my last memo I enclose the revised management structure scenarios as approved by the rationalisation committee, together with the minutes of the last sub-committee meeting.

You will note the committee still requires the financial information. When is a good time to collect this? I need hardly remind you that time is an issue.

——

Mike,

Have you received anything from NG? I haven't seen a thing, and neither has Jack. The man must have done something by now. We should have the phones working by tomorrow.

Mike,

Thanks for the P & L input. It is very useful (as was
Jack's – you should have received your copy). Have
you had anything yet from NG? I'm thinking of sending
another reminder. If you could send one as well he might
respond to one of us. The phones are still not working
here.

———

To: N. Grayford

From: S. DeMont

The rationalisation committee has asked me to remind
you that the financial reports have not yet been received.
Could you let me know when you are likely to have
this information? I can call at your office on Thursday
afternoon to collect.

———

Mike,

I'm sending this handwritten note because the phones
are out again. It's just to say I've sent another memo to NG
re the missing figures. It really would be useful if you
could send him a reminder as well. I've already spoken to
Jack.

To: N. Grayford

From: S. DeMont

I was disappointed on visiting your office to find that
the information was still not available. I would have
liked to meet you in person to discuss this but your staff
informed me they did not know your whereabouts or
when you were likely to return. Can I remind you that this
request is an *important* matter. We will not be able to
make a case for the restructuring if we do not have this
basic information.

———

Mike,

My note was not in any way intended as a reproach.
Nobody appreciates your hard work for the committee
as much as I do. It's just that NG is our biggest single
obstacle and some pressure from Parks and Libraries
might be useful. Jack is doing what he can on behalf of
T & E. Given the nature of NG's position vis-à-vis the
council it's probably best we work together on this. My
apologies for any misunderstanding.

———

Mike,

I'm sure that you are, as you say, 'well aware of the
situation' as regards NG. Once again, my original note
was intended as a friendly request for help rather than an
attack on your position. We are, I think, on the same side
here, and will need to work together if the restructuring
is to be viable.

I have had a reply from NG, though not one containing any actual information. I haven't yet decided if I should reply at all. Have you had any contact with him yourself?

———

To: N. Grayford

From: S. DeMont

Thank you for your reply. I would remind you that standard stationery is to be used for all official correspondence, and that having a handwritten note delivered to my private address at 1.15 on a Sunday morning is outside council policy. Furthermore, 'I'm working on it, so get off my back' is not acceptable as an explanation for the continuing delay.

Your note has been placed on file.

———

Mike,

Once again, my request was not intended to 'undermine your position'. I really can't see how you think it was. I'm sorry to hear you're too busy to arrange a meeting. I assure you I don't have much 'time on my hands' myself.

In answer to your question, yes, Jack has offered to apply additional pressure on NG through informal channels in his own department. Please do not interpret this as a conspiracy against you.

Mike,

The fact that Jack's wife works in the same department as myself really does not mean that we are engaged in a conspiracy against you. As it happens, I hardly know the woman. (Between ourselves, she isn't the friendliest person in the department.) The restructuring is an issue that should be more important than interdepartmental politics. If we can't control or at least influence it, it could have serious implications for all of us, and I, for one, don't want to be on the losing side. We simply cannot allow NG's intransigence to drag us down with him – we don't have his lifebelt, after all. I feel that your current objections are based on a misunderstanding that could easily be resolved in a face-to-face meeting.

———

To: N. Grayford

From: S. DeMont

I called at your office yesterday and found that not only were you not there, but you hadn't been there for the past week. Your staff were still unable to account for your absence, and had been left with no instructions. Are you any closer to providing the required information?

———

Mike,

I was glad we were finally able to meet and discuss the issues. I found it very productive, and would definitely be in favour of scheduling more meetings on a regular basis. I'm glad you now appreciate that I am not your enemy. (You do appreciate that, don't you?)

I think you are right to question the usefulness of informal approaches where NG is concerned. Yes, the best result would be to have him removed from the sub-committee, or from the finance department altogether. However, I think we should give him one more chance before we approach the rationalisation committee.

———

To: N. Grayford

From: S. DeMont

Thank you for your memo. With regard to the points you raise:

1) I will not name the staff member who advised me of your extended absence.

2) I have referred your comments re the process management department to that department. Their response is attached. Note especially their offer to provide evidence their systems were available on the dates in question.

3) I am pleased that you are offering to take this dispute, as you call it, to Councillor Grayford. I would remind you that the councillor is the chair of the rationalisation committee and has expressed his unreserved support for the proposed reallocation of resources. As the only delay to the implementation of the proposal is down to the non-provision of financial information I am sure he would welcome the opportunity for personal intervention.

Please let me know by return when the required information will be available.

—

Mike,

I've received another reply from NG, once again without any of the required information. I've sent copies to you and Jack. I think it's now clear we're not going to get anything useful from him, and should try another approach.

I can make half an hour tomorrow at 2.15. The same place?

—

M,

Yes, I wish the meeting could have lasted longer as well. It was still productive! What is missing from so much council work is precisely that personal touch.

I think the new approach to NG will be the correct one. Working through diplomacy, informal channels, etc., has failed.

Will you be free tomorrow to discuss? I have a meeting, but I can always cancel.

To: N. Grayford

From: S. DeMont

I refer to my memo of last week and note we have still not received a reply. I have now referred this matter to ~~your uncle~~ Councillor Grayford.

———

M,

I've done as we agreed. It will be interesting to see what happens now. Jack's informal channels have turned out not to be particularly useful – not that I think Jack has been pushing particularly hard. He probably doesn't want to rock the boat, especially as there's yet another Grayford nephew who's obviously being groomed for his job. I wish we could adopt your other suggestion! It's strange to think that ten years ago we could have done it without a second thought. I suppose we should be grateful we can't any more – it's a sign of progress, rule of law, and all that. The important thing now is to focus on the restructuring. It's the councillor's project, and I suspect it is more important to him than the welfare of NG.

———

To: N. Grayford

From: S. DeMont

I have received your most recent memo and would make the following observations:

1) You are supposed to be a senior officer within the finance department. Providing financial information at the request of department managers is part of your job description. I understand Councillor Grayford has approached you privately concerning this.

2) Once again I have forwarded your comments regarding the computer systems to the PM team.

I look forward to your prompt response.

———

M,

I waited for you for an hour yesterday. Is something wrong? You could have phoned me in the afternoon (the phones, for once, were working for most of the day). I can't tell you how often I think of what could happen, but I suppose we always fear the worst because of how we grew up. I know we've had ten years of peace and all that, but there are still so many unforeseeable circumstances that we can't, at times, help feeling anxious. Please let me know what happened.

I've had another reply from NG. I think he's rattled. I will accept your offer of additional protection. (Audit can't approve anything until I receive an explicit threat, and won't interpret anything NG does as threatening. And, to be honest, I think they're right. He's not a man you take seriously.)

I think we are a good example of interdepartmental co-operation!

M,

I was glad to hear nothing was seriously wrong. You know how rumours spread in this town. I'm sorry you weren't able to come, but glad it was just because of work.

I've finally spoken to you-know-who about our Finance problem. He wasn't happy, but finally agreed NG isn't right for the job. He'll be gone as soon as they can find another sinecure for him. It's a good thing for us that MG puts his plans for the authority above his plans for his family.

There's a price, however. MG wants a simpler management structure for the new transport department. I haven't yet discussed the implications of this with Jack – it's something I'd like to talk to you about first. But we have to proceed carefully here. We don't want to overcome one obstacle in Finance only to find we have another in Jack. This is something we need to discuss, and soon. Tomorrow, at twelve?

Denise

Denise worked on basement Level D in the main council building. Below her were the interview rooms Audit shared with Welfare; below that was Level F, which Denise knew housed the emergency generators; she also knew, in the uncertain way most things about the council were known, that people were sometimes taken there from interview rooms. The level below F did not have an official designation: council workers sometimes called it 'the pit' or 'the bunker'. It was supposed to have been designed as a bomb shelter and was now a storeroom for old documents. Denise had never been to that level; few people in her department had. It belonged to the Historical Records Office and Denise worked for Current Records.

Outsiders – even Jack, who should have known better – talked as if Audit was a single monolithic entity. The staff knew it was as riven with factions as any other department of the council. HRO were traditionally Conservative and regarded CRO as unnecessary – *all* records, in their view, were historical, and the CRO was no more than a legacy of the Labour ascendancy. CRO staff, for their part, despised the HRO as hoarders who wanted control of all records without any idea how to use them: HRO's information retrieval was a standing joke in CRO, just as the incompleteness of CRO's records was a standing joke in HRO. The disagreements were at their worst near Archive Dates, when old CRO files were transferred to HRO. The next date was three months ahead, and already the memoranda were flying, CRO claiming it was authorised to keep records for twelve years, HRO claiming the limit was ten, and both sides remembering the time when HRO had sent an armed team to collect some disputed files only to be met by a larger armed team from CRO. Although HRO had backed down on that occasion, both sides remembered how close they had come to an *incident*. Denise hadn't seen it for herself – the confrontation had taken place on C Level – but had heard different accounts, some from people who claimed to have been there. She had been careful not to ask too many questions: Audit employees were supposed to be well informed, but the wrong kind of curiosity could end a career, and Denise did not want to be seen taking an excessive interest in anything beyond the papers that crossed her desk. She belonged to the faction that tried to ignore politics, which in practice meant not engaging in small talk or expressing opinions, and listening to other people's opinions without saying anything. This suited her; at work, she wanted to disappear into her job, to be both unobtrusive and necessary.

She worked with her back to the wall in a cramped office – they were all cramped offices, divided and subdivided, with flimsy partition walls bolstered by filing cabinets – next to Record Room 4. There was a narrow passageway between her desk and the desk assigned to her assistant. All through the day workers from the adjoining offices would file past, carrying armfuls of folders to and from the record room, occasionally stopping with release forms for Denise to authorise. Between eight and six most of her day was made up of interruptions; most of her work was done when the junior staff had left.

There was a ventilation shaft behind her assistant's desk. When it worked the fan would rattle and clank as if it was about to break down. When it didn't work the room became hot and airless. That day it wasn't working. By half past ten Denise felt as if she was covered with a film of sweat.

She stared at the open file on her desk. She had been looking through it for the last half-hour without taking in a single word. In the same time she had signed four release forms about which, minutes later, she could not remember a single detail. From time to time she turned the pages in front of her so that anyone passing would think she was actually studying them. Denise believed she had worked there long enough to be trusted; she outranked all but two other people on her floor. None of the staff who carried files past her desk had the authority to question her, yet she still kept up the pretence.

She found it hard to work in the mornings. Until about half past ten her mind was clouded. She would read a report and realise she had not understood a word. When she tried to formulate sentences, she found the language itself was recalcitrant, or lost in a kind of fog. She wondered if this was an effect of alcohol. Yet it had been years since she'd last drunk enough on a weekday evening to induce that kind of pain. There had been a time when everybody she knew drank heavily; when, looking back, it seemed as if the whole town had been drunk – drunk and armed, spoiling for a fight and finding one, again and again. The disturbances were supposed to have been about politics or food, but really they were an extended drunken brawl, when the town was split between rival factions of drunks, a rivalry complicated by the factions of the self-righteously teetotal, many of whom had once been drunks. Somehow she had survived that time, and now drank only on Friday and Saturday nights, and occasionally on Sundays. During the week Jack still had two glasses of whisky before retiring (when they had whisky); Denise would drink nothing stronger than herb tea. Yet every morning Jack was the one who swung out of bed, alert and energetic and already in a bad mood, while she struggled towards consciousness, often not knowing what day it was and with a sense that she'd forgotten how to read. There were mornings when she wondered if she hadn't suffered some kind of unnoticed head injury, or if there was a tumour burgeoning behind the centre of her forehead, at the point of her recurring, methodical ache. There had to be a physical explanation for this decline: early senility perhaps, or the cumulative effect of years when she had drunk every night.

The file on her desk was on Perry Tunstall, described on the request form as 'a local businessman, known associate of Henderson'. The request form was from Councillor Braddon.

A request from a councillor was always political: they would be looking either for damaging information about an opponent or for reassurance about a proposed business partner. If the subject was described as an associate of

Henderson it meant they wanted something damaging. Denise was good at knowing what could be released. Information was slippery stuff. Once out of their vaults it could end up anywhere, be used for any purpose. Information about Subject X could incriminate Subject Y, or be combined with information about Subject M in a way that could embarrass whoever raised the original request. It was an Audit principle to release as little of it as possible, just in case. Denise owed her position to her sense of what was appropriate. She was careful. It could make people angry, but they usually knew better than to complain.

Perry Tunstall's file was unremarkable. The phone transcripts were from two years earlier and consisted of three pages of calls, none to or from Henderson. Either his involvement was recent or Perry Tunstall was a careful man, or Councillor Braddon had made a mistake. There were two inconclusive police reports from the year before the last transcript, and seventeen denunciations, all anonymous, concerned with smuggling either contraband in or people out. Twelve of the seventeen denunciations seemed to be from the same source. Denise read through the documents again, waiting for her impressions to coalesce into actual thoughts. She wondered if the information in the file was enough to justify asking for an Expedited Transcript from the telecommunications room. It was a question of money: a transcript could take a council stenographer days and produce nothing of value – or nothing a councillor could use. Audit would have to pay, while not receiving its percentage of Tunstall's estate. Denise hesitated. Her ability to make this kind of decision was the basis of her career – she knew this, because other managers often asked her for advice. She usually told them the same thing: investigate further. Everybody, it was believed, had broken at least one rule. The only question was whether the offence merited the time and expense required to bring it to light, though Denise was occasionally haunted by the idea that one day she would initiate an inquiry into somebody who had done absolutely nothing wrong.

It seemed unlikely that person would be Perry Tunstall. He seemed to have money without having worked for the council, usually a clear indication of something that could be interpreted as criminal activity. But that morning Denise looked at the documents in his file and wondered. At any other time of day she could make a decision in seconds; before eleven she was helpless. She reread the denunciations. They were not enough, she decided. The police reports might have been sufficient – if only she could interpret them. For now, the documents seemed to make no sense. She was relieved when her phone rang.

Switchboard told her it was a call from Amex. She expected it to be Siobhan, the only person from Amex who had ever called her. It was a man's voice. 'Denise? It's Tim.'

At first she didn't recognise the voice. She nearly asked: *Tim who?* Then she realised: it was Louise's Tim, a friend, or the husband of a friend. A quiet, dry man, whose voice on the phone sounded determined and apologetic. 'What do you want, Tim?' She tried to sound forbidding. You weren't supposed to use official lines for private calls. She didn't want whoever was listening to think she was encouraging him.

Tim, to his credit, sounded as if he understood the rules. 'I have an enquiry concerning a file request.'

So this was an official call. 'There are official channels for that kind of information.'

'Understood. But this is in the nature of a preliminary enquiry.'

In the nature of. The official periphrasis. Telephone conversations could sound as stilted as dialogues in a language lesson, as if you were being marked on vocabulary and grammar. 'I see.'

'We do want access to a file.' Tim sounded calm. She wondered if he'd written down what he needed to say. 'However, to speed things up we'd like to determine in advance what level of clearance is necessary.'

'I see.'

'Would you be able to give me some indication?' There was no warmth in his voice.

But then there was none in hers. 'That will depend on the nature of the request.'

There was a pause, the faintest suggestion of a smile. 'I appreciate your assistance.'

'Not all of our files will be available for non-council ...' There was a word she meant to use and couldn't, somehow, remember. It was a word she used every day. She tried 'consideration'. It seemed to fit.

'That's understood.' Tim sounded so neutral she wondered for a moment if this was Louise's Tim or simply someone with a similar voice, another Tim she might have met once and forgotten, calling from another department to check up ('Tell her you're from Amex ...'). He'd report back on her deviation from standard procedures. 'She made no attempt to identify me ...' Her career would be over. 'Part of the reason for making this preliminary enquiry,' the voice continued, 'is to determine whether the information is available. Or if there is a file at all.'

'What is the subject's name?'

'It's a Parks employee.'

'Then there will be a file.' It seemed odd to be having this conversation with Tim. But then she had never really known what he did at work. 'Can I ask the reason for this request?'

'We'd rather not disclose it at this stage.'

'We will need a reason before we can release any information.'

'Of course. Under what circumstances would the council release this kind of information? We would not want the request to be denied on a technicality.'

Denise admired his tenacity. 'Information will be released if it is considered to be in the interests of the council.'

'Would co-operation with us be considered in its interests?'

'Possibly.' A clerk leaned over her desk with an armful of folders. Denise waved her away. 'The council may define its interests more narrowly than you expect. A lot will depend on whose file is requested.'

'I see.' Tim hesitated, as if consulting a list. Then he said, 'It's Kieran Leith.'

'Who?'

'Leith,' Tim repeated. 'Kieran Leith.'

That Kieran. Siobhan's Kieran. The only person called Kieran she had ever met or heard of. Of course it was him.

Why would Amex be interested in Kieran? There were the negotiations over the stadium – still called a stadium despite its being years since any sport had been held there. But the names persisted long after the uses had changed:

there was a command post by the seafront that was still called the Aquarium, and a holding block on West Street still referred to as the Ice Rink. Perhaps Amex was looking for leverage, a weapon they could use against Parks, and believed Kieran was involved in something illegal.

Ridiculous. Kieran was in Parks. Of course he was involved in something illegal.

'Denise, are you still there?'

'I'm still here.' She dismissed her thoughts. Speculation was a bad habit. 'Why are you asking for this?'

'As I said, we have our reasons.'

'No, I mean why are *you* asking? I'd have expected to receive enquiries through your security division.'

'This is just a preliminary enquiry. Security will take over once we know the appropriate level.'

'I see. This is unorthodox.' Wheels within wheels. 'I'll see what I can do.'

'I appreciate this, Denise.' He corrected himself: 'That is, we appreciate this.'

He hung up. Denise listened to the buzz on the line for a few seconds before she replaced the receiver.

The clerk with the folders had gone. Perry Tunstall's file was still meaningless. She could think only about Tim's request. Why Kieran? Denise knew him only as Siobhan's husband, friendly enough across a dinner table, but dull; a man who deflected questions about his past and mentioned people only to praise them. Empty, she'd decided, and harmlessly insincere. One of Alan's jokes was to ask him, 'So how many people have you killed this week?' 'Oh,' he'd shrug, and try to play along, 'you know, the usual number.' It was a nervous joke, because there was always the suspicion that his job really was dirtier than he could say. Parks, after all, cultivated a reputation for brutal efficiency. It didn't matter that, if the reports that crossed her desk were to be believed, the reputation was undeserved: that their brutality was largely a matter of off-duty pub brawls with Transport, and their efficiency confined mainly to their co-operation with smugglers. Kieran didn't take part in the brawls and if he was involved in the corruption he had little to show for it; but then the other joke about him, the one they didn't say to his face, was that he was tight-fisted. It was said that the smartest clothes he owned were his uniforms; that, when he came to dinner, he always brought the cheapest wine, the bottle that had to be drunk last, when it couldn't be pushed to one side and forgotten. Alan had repeated this once, to his face; Kieran's silence had been more laughable than ominous. Louise had later claimed she'd thought he was about to cry, though that had been, as usual with Louise, an exaggeration. Kieran was a good-natured if absurd person tolerated because the others seemed to like Siobhan. What was behind Tim's request now? Had Siobhan revealed something about him? Or was Siobhan herself under suspicion?

This, Denise thought, was more likely than Tim showing any concern for Siobhan. They didn't, as far as she knew, even work in the same office. Siobhan had once said she was more likely to see Tim in one of their houses than at work. And Louise, exaggerating, but not by much, routinely referred to her husband as a cold fish.

Denise went on shuffling through Perry Tunstall's file. If Amex was behind Tim's request then it was likely they weren't interested in Kieran except as a representative of Parks. There was the outstanding issue of the stadium purchase. Tim may have offered up his Audit contact to improve his own prospects. This might have nothing to do with Siobhan or Kieran or Tim. This could even be about Amex testing Audit itself ...

She could feel her head clear. It would soon be time to start working properly. She put down Perry Tunstall's file and wrote 'No significant information currently held – Expedited Transcript requested' on the councillor's blue request form. It was a decision that delayed having to make a decision. Something would turn up.

She looked over at her assistant's desk. She hadn't had an assistant for three months – the post was being kept open 'for strategic reasons', meaning, in case a councillor had to find a job for somebody quickly. In those three months the desk had become a repository for files she consulted regularly. She sidled round her desk and pulled out the most recent Records Held Index, a foot-thick printout on pale green fanfold. She found Kieran's file number and went into Records Room 4.

Excuse my not typing this note. Am writing this with my left hand to preserve my identity. (I am NOT left handed). I have important information regarding ———. He is a thief and a liar. He said he could get A FRIEND of mine a job in FRANCE. He goes to pubs and tells people he knows people in FRANCE who want to give jobs to English people because we will work for less. MY FRIEND believed him and gave him the money that was necessary but when MY FRIEND got to FRANCE he found that there was no work and MY FRIEND was left in that camp near DIEPPE which the papers have written about. He was there for TWO MONTHS. He has not been able to find work since and has been living on SCRAPS he finds on the ground at the OPEN MARKET. THIS IS ALL THE FAULT OF ——— ———. Have writ to police but they do nothing. Hope you can do SOMETHING. If not for MY FRIEND then for OTHER PEOPLE.

———

A FRIEND of mine who was in a PUB on the LEWES ROAD tells me that he heard ————— is still telling people he can find them jobs in FRANCE. This is a lie as I know from MY FRIEND who made the mistake of BELIEVING him. There was no work and he spent THREE MONTHS in a camp near DIEPPE (I cannot spell the name). Where the conditions were appalling. MY FRIEND has not been able to find work and it is only because of the HELMSTONE MISSION that he is able to eat one hot meal a day. He is truly a PITIFUL sight and it is all the fault of ————— . I think you should make this known to people so he is unable to TRICK people again. You could put posters in PUBS that would be a good idea. Excuse not typing. I am writing this with my left hand so you will not know who I am.

———

Last week I was told by A FRIEND who drinks in the ————— PUB that ————— is still making his lies about work in FRANCE. He is also smuggling CIGARETTES and foreign BEER which he sells to the PUBS. You must write to people or put up posters to tell people not to LISTEN to him he is telling LIES. He takes money and then you spend SIX MONTHS in DIEPPE where you are treated like you are a CRIMINAL this is what happened to A FRIEND. Since he came back he has been living with other friends until they asked him to leave because he has no MONEY and now he is staying at the HELMSTONE MISSION but it is very crowded. ONE POUND would make a lot of difference. You must put up posters to tell people the TRUTH about ————. I have writ to you before but this will be my last letter as I have used up this pen.

————

I am writing to say it would be GOOD if you can do something to help the HELMSTONE MISSION. They are GOOD people who do GOOD work. For eg MY FRIEND was treated by them very well when he came back from FRANCE where he was treated very badly because of the LIES of ————. They have given him a bed and a new pen but it is very crowded and the hymn singing is in the same room he sleeps in which means he does not sleep enough and this is affecting his MIND. A FEW POUNDS would make all the difference now that he has TURNED AWAY from drink. HELMSTONE MISSION are GOOD people. Yours in JESUS.

————

I did not sign my last letter because I want to preserve my identity and I will not sign this one for the same reason as ———— is still telling his LIES and because at night he MY FRIEND is trying to SLEEP and the other people are singing the hymns and sometimes FIGHTING over the soup and ———— is trying to have MY FRIEND told to leave the MISSION he goes to the MISSION at night and laughs at MY FRIEND and when MY FRIEND tells the people at the MISSION that ———— is there they tell him he is WRONG and that he must stop SHOUTING. They are GOOD people but they do not know that ———————— is still in the PUBS and MY FRIEND has seen him even though MY FRIEND does not drink. You must do something to stop him.

———

This is the VOICE of one crying in the WILDNESS.

———

Excuse this writing. I am using my left hand for reasons of and it is late at night. Know that in the last days PERILOUS times will come and we ARE living in the last days as is shown by many SIGNS. By the MERCY of Lord JESUS Christ my SAVOUR I have come at last to this place of refuge safe at last from the temptation of drink and the lies of ————————. I pray for his SOUL though he is an evil man who offers men DRINK until they agree to work for him as I have seen for myself MY FRIEND listened to his lies. He tells people he is not to be believed but they LAUGH at him and the pubs are PART of his wickedness. They buy their drink from him it is landed on the BEACH at night as I MY FRIEND has seen and when he told the guards they said Go away and I can't see anything and laughed. They do not see the EVIL in their souls they are not write with GOD so I write again though it is slow with my left hand. I PRAY for you.

———

Excuse writing but my hand is painful after two nights ago. I am writing to tell how MY FRIEND was about his work of telling the evil of ———————— when he saw him in a PUB drinking and laughing with his friends or people who THOUGHT he was their friend I should say. MY FRIEND then went to him saying Remember me and told him of the time spent in DIEPPE because of his lies. And ———————— was downcast which made MY FRIEND stop and ———————— said I did not know and I have been badly let down. And he said to MY FRIEND You are the one they talk about the one who calls me a liar. And MY FRIEND said Yes, because you said there was work and I was kept in a CAMP. And ———————— said There has been a terrible understanding and How can I make this up to you. And MY FRIEND told him he was staying with the HELMSTONE MISSION who were GOOD people and needed HELP and perhaps ———————— could help them. And ———————— said You must show me where this is and MY FRIEND said Yes. But when they had left the pub and were in the street ———————— laughed at MY FRIEND and started to hit MY FRIEND saying Don't come to one of my pubs and If I see you again it will be worse. He kicked MY FRIEND when he was on the ground and now MY FRIEND has pains in his chest and it is HARD to write and the MISSION are GOOD people but say he must leave because he is drinking and FIGHTING. They are GOOD people but they do not listen and that is why you should

Louise

This time it was Jack sitting in Louise's kitchen, drinking her tea and keeping her from working. People stopped by in the afternoons as if what she did couldn't be important because it was done at a kitchen table. Unlike Alan, Jack didn't give a reason for his visit. He just turned up with the air of someone bringing urgent news and then stayed to make small talk, so Louise mentioned her suspicions about Tim. Jack seemed to find his behaviour outrageous. 'No,' he said, his brow furrowed as if he'd expected anything but this. 'I haven't heard anything about any plans. But then Tim doesn't exactly confide in me either.' He sat stiffly, his dark three-piece suit – like something you'd wear to a funeral – looking absurdly formal in the untidy domesticity of her kitchen, cradling a mug as if he expected it to be snatched from him at any moment. Jack was an awkward man. Denise had once claimed any oddities of his behaviour – or most of them anyway – could be traced back to his being from a large, competitive family where you grabbed what food you could get and held on to it until it was eaten. Or, Louise thought, it might

110

be that Jack was simply odd and would have been odd whatever his childhood. 'In fact,' he said, as carefully as if he was presenting his findings to a committee, 'I haven't spoken to Tim since that dinner at Alan's, the night of the accident.'

Odd and absent-minded. 'Come on, Jack, you've seen him at least twice since then.' Louise would have liked to ask if *accident* was going to be the official version. Once she could have asked that kind of question and Jack would have been bitter and amusing. That morning he was morose, which at least meant he was too tired to be angry. He and Denise both worked sixty- or seventy-hour weeks: anything, Louise thought, to avoid each other's company. 'You even talked to him at the last one, and that was only a week ago. About why Amex taking over the stadium was a bad idea, I seem to remember.'

'Did I?' Jack frowned. Except you couldn't really say he frowned. You had to say his frown deepened, or he frowned more. He gazed at the wet clothes on her airing rack as if he disapproved of the way they were hung. 'I don't remember that. And it is a bad idea. I don't know why he doesn't understand that.'

'He agreed with you. And then you talked about Doug and Sarah.'

'No wonder I've forgotten.' Even Jack's attempts at humour were sour. 'I was just grateful Alan and Margaret weren't arguing again.'

'You have this idea they argue all the time.'

'Because they do. Even when there's not a knock-down drag-out row there's usually some bickering in corners.'

'No more than anyone else.' She wondered about his vehemence. Was there trouble at work? Or had he reached

111

the point where he was now angry about everything? 'No more than you and Denise.'

He was startled. 'We do not.'

'Come on, Jack. You might think you save it till you're in the car, but most times you've started before you've left the house. Sometimes you're arguing when you arrive. Don't worry about it. Most couples argue. If they're still talking to each other.'

'Rubbish.' Then he sounded less certain. 'Do you and Tim? Argue?'

'We don't talk enough to argue. How's Denise?'

Jack's mind was elsewhere. 'Alan and Margaret *do* argue all the time. You must have seen that. You've seen it, haven't you?' Before she could reply he said, as if in answer to his own question: 'I don't like Alan.'

'Really.' Louise wondered, not for the first time, why Jack was in her kitchen. Alan came with invitations; Jack just showed up, as if he'd had a bad morning and expected to be entertained. 'Doesn't that make things awkward at work?'

'He's all right to work with. He's a good worker. It's just' – he looked at her, as if not sure how she'd react – 'I don't trust him. Socially.'

'Why not? The Grayford thing?'

'No. It's not that. Well, partly it is. I mean, that's not something you ignore, is it? No. There's more to it than that ...' He trailed off, helplessly.

'Jack, I don't know what you mean.'

He looked at her as if he'd expected her to say more, and was taken aback that she didn't. 'I don't like the way he treats Margaret.'

Stranger and stranger. Alan and Margaret were the self-consciously golden couple. Everything they did – their mutual deference, their careful avoidance of any public disagreement, the way Margaret never complained about any aspect of her partner's frequently annoying behaviour even when given a clear opportunity – seemed designed to show how well matched they were. 'I really don't think Margaret is concerned.'

'Well, she should be.'

'Why?'

'The way he flirts. Right in front of her.' Jack was almost squirming in his seat – if someone so rigid could be said to squirm. 'I don't think that's fair.'

'Who does he flirt with?' Another strange idea. Alan was too earnest to flirt. To flirt, you had to notice the other person. You had to flatter them, pay them attention. Alan took himself too seriously for any of that. 'I've never seen him flirt.'

'Oh, you must have. I mean, the last time, in his own home, with Margaret right there.' Jack was wide-eyed. He even put down his mug and spread his arms in a gesture of incredulity. 'I don't see how you could miss it.'

'I was talking to him for most of the evening. I didn't notice any flirting.'

'That's what I'm talking about.' In a matter of seconds Jack went from being angry to being flustered, and then to an uncharacteristic contrition. 'It's just that I think marriage is a commitment, and when you've made it you shouldn't ...' He trailed off again, ending weakly with: 'You don't flirt. You shouldn't flirt.'

'You think Alan was flirting?'

'What else was he doing?'

'He was talking about himself. He was saying, "Like me, like me, I'm a good person." That's not flirting.'

He snapped: 'Sometimes that's all it takes.'

'What do you mean, Jack?' She had to remind herself that he didn't mean to be rude. That, at least, was the excuse Denise sometimes made for him. Louise thought this was too indulgent. Jack was not a child. 'Are you saying married men shouldn't talk to married women? Like we're doing now?'

'That's not the point. I'm not Alan.'

'So it's just Alan who shouldn't talk to other women?'

Jack twitched, grimaced, and seemed suddenly ready to start shouting. He managed to ratchet his voice down from angry to merely aggrieved but it was a close-run thing. 'Look, when you put it like that you make it sound as if I'm not being rational.'

'That's because you aren't.' Louise considered the files spread across her table. Why did people always come to her? She already knew, or could guess, the answer: because, in their little circle, Margaret would be unsympathetic, Sarah too busy, Denise too forbidding (and, in Jack's case, too familiar), and Siobhan too wrapped up in her own little world ... So she was the one they interrupted and whose time they wasted. 'Why don't you like Alan? What has he done to hurt you?'

'It's not that I don't like him.' Jack sounded appalled she could think such a thing. 'I do. He's good to work with. It's just – it's just that I don't trust him.'

She laughed. 'And I'd ask why you don't trust him. Except you'd probably say it's because you don't like him.'

'I've never said I don't like him.'

'You did.'

'I didn't. I've never said that.'

114

'You did. Five minutes ago, sitting at this very table, you said: "I don't like Alan."'

'Well, those might have been my words, but it's hardly what I meant.'

'Jack, what did you mean?'

'Let me think about this.' He held out his arms and flexed his fingers as if trying to disentangle them from something sticky. 'I don't want to say something and have you misquote me.'

'Jack, when I repeat something you say it's called *quoting*.'

'You know what I mean. I suppose what I was trying to say is that it comes down to a question of principles.'

'So you don't like Alan on principle?'

For a moment she thought she'd gone too far and he was going to walk out of the kitchen, never to return. She felt an immediate impulse to apologise, which she resisted. It was unfair how Jack could make you feel responsible for his own lack of proportion. But difficult people were like that: difficult because they were given too much latitude, and given too much latitude because they were difficult – which made them more difficult ... She tried to imagine Jack as a younger man, a wild-eyed figure striding the Downs, choking with rage at every turn. Louise could see how that kind of angry idealism might appeal to someone like Denise. But give your Heathcliff twenty years in a compromising day job; watch that exacting morality decline into peevishness ... Louise liked Jack, or the idea of Jack; she thought she knew what made him tick – the same clockwork that made him go off at regular intervals.

This time he managed to control himself. To be fair, he always did. It was just that lately he gave the impression that he was one disagreement away from losing his temper and never getting it back. Then he would join the other men his age who wandered the street, shouting or muttering at the unfairness of the world. Most of these other men were poorer than Jack, and uneducated; they had never been anything, or had succeeded briefly, when they were young, before being pushed aside; now they drank whatever they could find, gathered on the Level at nights, and waited for the end of the world. Louise had worked with them; she had read the meagre biographies in their files: when she looked at Jack she recognised a type.

But Jack wasn't ready to join them yet. For now, though it cost him an effort, he could sound reasonable, if unhappy. 'I don't think this is a laughing matter. People who are married ought to live according to certain standards of behaviour. This includes not flirting, as you call it, with other women. A marriage is a commitment to the other person, and that commitment means refraining from doing anything that could upset them. And Alan doesn't display that commitment and that's why I don't like Alan. Disapprove, rather. You know what I mean.'

She waited until she was certain he had finished. 'Alan's not married.'

'What?'

'Alan and Margaret aren't married.'

'That's a technicality. They have a commitment.'

'How do you know?'

'Well, they ought to have a commitment. And I don't think Alan honours it.'

'So you don't like him socially.' She wondered about his real objection. It was probably something to do with work. Was she concerned enough to find out? 'But you don't mind him at work. You know, it's usually the other way round. How's Denise?'

'He's not so bad at work.' Jack blinked at his wife's name. 'I mean, he does what I tell him, and that's the main thing. This one-way system again – more bloody politics. I've given most of that to Alan. It's the sort of thing he's good at. Out of the whole family he's the only one you'd employ because he's good at his job. At least, he's better than that useless bloody cousin of his.'

'That's who Alan was talking about when you thought he was flirting.' Comparing himself to the man, she remembered; naturally the comparison had been to Alan's advantage.

'That clown?' Talking about somebody else, Jack sounded reasonable. Or, rather, his anger became appropriate. 'He's been kicked sideways. Out of Finance, into Personnel. There was some talk of him going to Parks. He's supposed to have pleaded with the old man not to be sent there. On his hands and knees, weeping, I heard, saying he wouldn't last five minutes, which I thought was the bloody idea. Anyway, the old man relented. Anybody else would have been sacked.'

'They made a new post for him?'

'Not quite. Some kid called Hoskiss was moved to Parks instead. Bit of a stink, as Hoskiss was a Labour pick. People had to be reassured he wasn't going front line. But it's typical.'

'At least Alan doesn't like his family. How's Denise?'

'The thing about Alan is, I don't think you can come from a family like his and not be influenced. I think things have come too easily for him.'

'You've just said he was good at his job. What does it matter how he got it?' For a moment, Jack looked startled, as if she'd said something so illogical he didn't know how to respond. Louise pressed on: 'I think the truth is you don't know why you don't like him. Nothing you've said has been a good reason. You seem determined to interpret everything he does in the worst possible light. I think you should stop worrying about him. Now, how's Denise?'

'See? You're twisting my words. I don't like him or dislike him. It's just I don't think he's to be trusted. You make it sound as if that's irrational.'

'I'm sorry, Jack, but I think you *are* irrational,' she said lightly, hoping he would take it as the friendly banter it only half was. 'And I've tried three times to make you change the subject. And now, so you don't miss it, for the fourth time, how is Denise?'

Jack looked down at his mug. 'Denise is fine.'

'You sound reluctant to talk about her.'

'No, no, I'm not reluctant,' he said, reluctantly. 'It's just that – Denise is fine. Audit is – there are no problems with Audit.'

'That's good.'

'I don't want to talk about Denise.'

'Jack, I'm going to be blunt. What's up with you? You've been preoccupied ever since you got here.'

'I don't know how you can say that.'

'Believe me, Jack, you're not acting normally. And I see a lot of what isn't normal in this town.'

'Russell Street scum.'

'They're not the only ones. You should get out of the office more. You haven't been able to say what you mean and you seem to be obsessed with Alan. If you're under a lot of pressure somewhere and don't want to talk about it, that's fine. Just don't think it hasn't been noticed.'

'I'm not obsessed with Alan. It's just that when I see him talking to people—'

'You assume the worst?'

'No. Yes.'

'You think he's flirting with other women in front of his – of Margaret?'

'When he was talking to you, yes.'

'All he was doing was what we're doing now, that's all. Just talking. I mean, would you call what we're doing now flirting?'

Jack grimaced, like a man forced to swallow poison. The answer came as a whisper: 'Yes.'

It was all she could do not to laugh in his face.

Present: Cllrs John Braddon, Theresa Harding, Geoffrey Plaice.

... a very moving affair.

Quite, Miss Harding.

It's a pity there were so few people.

Well, the late councillor was a controversial figure. If we had made it a more public event, there was a danger we would attract the wrong kind of attention.

I dunno. Might have livened things up.

Now, Geoff.

At least I stayed awake. More than you can say for Grayford. What happened to him, anyway? Isn't he supposed to be here as well?

I really think you should show more respect, Mr Plaice.

I'll show respect where it's due. I just don't think it's due to Grayford. Or Goss, for that matter. I don't know why we bothered having a memorial service for the old bastard.

Whatever his faults, Mr Plaice—

And he had plenty of those.

The service was my idea, Mr Plaice. I know you have a low opinion of Mr Goss, but his devotion to the church would have surprised you.

It certainly would. So where is Grayford?

He had other business, Geoff.

Typical. Don't suppose you know what it was?

He's meeting Brierly from Parks.

Brierly? Isn't he the one carrying on with the bint from Audit?

I don't think that's what the meeting's about, Geoff.

Have you seen the woman? I wouldn't—

Mr Plaice! Please.

Each to his own, I suppose. So what is this other meeting about?

No idea, Geoff.

Up to no good, then.

You complain when Miles is present, Mr Plaice. You can hardly complain at his absence.

I bloody well can. At least when he's here I can keep an eye on him.

He has given me some notes.

Notes. Has he. Who does he think he is?

Please, Geoff.

OK, OK. Tell us what he has to say.

It's about the report on the Goss incident. The first draft of the final version. Have you both had a chance to read it?

This morning, before the service.

Geoff?

I glanced at it in church.

Mr Plaice, you could have pretended to show some respect.

I needed something to stop me from laughing.

Right, so you've both seen it. What did you think?

Looked all right to me. Nothing too sensational.

Well, Grayford wants a few changes.

Why does that not surprise me?

Actually, Geoff, I agree with him. He feels the scope of the report should be limited. He's given me these notes about the changes he feels we should insist on. Remember, any delay in producing the report will be useful.

So he's had time to make notes? When did he see the report?

Probably before we did. He has contacts within the force, you know.

Another nephew, I suppose.

It need not be, Mr Plaice. As the book says, he is smoother than oil.

Quite, Miss Harding. Anyway, here are the changes. Firstly, any reference to the councillor playing chicken to be removed completely, along with any reference to the driver's alleged former nickname—

Tyrone had a nickname?

Apparently so, when he was younger. The Chicken King.

No wonder he was such a miserable bastard. I'd say leave it in. Give it a bit of colour.

Grayford wants it out, Geoff. The chicken is speculation, and, where is it, the driver – here, the driver's old nickname is not relevant to this case.

It's relevant if it killed him.

We don't know that it did, Geoff. Anyway, that's Grayford's first point and I think it's a good one. Miss Harding?

I agree with Miles. There is no need to stain the memory of the deceased.

Agreed then. This is his second point. All references to a possible political or personal motive on the part of the other driver should be removed. As the other driver has left no account of his motives and is now unavailable for questioning, his motives cannot be known with certainty; speculation as to what they might have been should not form part of the report. Geoff?

Fair enough.

He also suggests that now the driver's identity has been established—

I missed that bit. How did they do that? I didn't think there was enough left of him.

It's here somewhere, you must have seen—

And since when did the police actually investigate anything? That's not what we pay them for.

The report says – here it is, seen in the vicinity of, description matches that of, yes, so it's eyewitnesses. He was seen.

No possibility of a mistake there, then.

They may be right, Geoff. Anyway, now that his identity has been established, Grayford says, where was I, it is appropriate to emphasise his various juvenile convictions.

So no double standard then.

Please, Geoff.

Oh, I'm not disagreeing. Carry on.

His relation to one of the children involved in an earlier incident involving Councillor Goss – please, Geoff, let me finish – is no more than a coincidence, and all references to the earlier incident should be removed. Miss Harding?

I was just remembering those poor children.

Quite. It was a, um, tragic accident. But I believe Grayford's right. There's no need to remind people about that aspect of—

It's all most people know about him.

They were unbaptised, poor things.

Still, as Grayford says, the councillor was exonerated at the time and the matter should now be regarded as closed.

Their poor souls, suffering in hell.

Can't be worse than anything they were used to.

Hell is not a joking matter, Mr Plaice.

Neither is Russell Street. And Russell Street exists.

As does hell, Mr Plaice.

I'll believe that when I see it.

[   ]

[   ]

Please, both of you. If we could get back to the business at hand. Grayford says, he says, I need hardly stress this is not the best time to remind the electorate about one of the more controversial aspects of the late councillor's career. The point we need to make is that the death of the councillor was an accident that proves we need to maintain stricter control of the roads.

Stricter control. Grayford all over.

He has a point, Geoff.

He has a plan, John. The man isn't going to be happy until he's made chancellor for life.

He's a shrewd operator, Geoff.

I fear he is not right with the Lord.

Few of us are, Miss Harding. Now, if I may go on to his third point. The subsequent events, including the shooting of the Barrows, should also be removed from the report as they are, strictly speaking, a separate matter entirely.

Let me get this straight, John. Grayford wants a report that doesn't include anything leading up to the accident, or anything that happened afterwards.

He has a point, Geoff. The business with the Barrows—

Wouldn't have happened without the accident.

Yes, but it's still a separate incident.

So what happens with the Barrows?

We'll negotiate a settlement with Mr Barrow. That shouldn't be too difficult. It turns out he's part of the compensation scheme.

I thought we'd cancelled that years ago.

Only for new entrants, Geoff. Anyway, it's a small price to pay if it means the Barrow case stays out of the election.

What is it Grayford says? We do not want the political process to be derailed by the personal misfortunes of individuals. That's what he says, and I'm inclined to agree with him. Geoff?

It can't do any harm. Mind you, how much harm can it do if we leave it as it is? How many people are going to see it anyway?

Well, the report itself isn't intended for circulation. But it will be seen by the international observers.

Blabbermouths.

Exactly. So we have to assume it will be widely circulated. Miss Harding?

I don't see why they have to see it. I mean, they simply don't understand our culture.

I appreciate you've had your disagreements—

They had the gall to complain about our gatherings to praise the Lord. They tried to stop my people from praying. Praying, Mr Braddon.

I think they were concerned you were trying to, ah, influence the vote. Perhaps your choice of venue—

I don't see why they should complain. My people stayed outside the polling station. Outside, Mr Braddon. These foreigners hate the Lord. I believe many of them are avowed Satanists.

That's putting it a little strongly, Miss Harding. Anyway, we need them. Without their support, we could find ourselves facing sanctions again. And the merest suggestion of a political assassination – Geoff?

I agree with you, John. I was just wondering how much this Barrow is going to cost us.

Whatever, it's a small price to pay for keeping him quiet.

I know cheaper ways.

We can't do that kind of thing any more, Geoff. We're a modern democratic society.

And it is, Mr Plaice, really the least we can do. The poor man lost his wife—

Probably a blessing in disguise. He should thank us. No, I'll go along with Grayford's changes. Let's get this election out of the way. I don't trust him, but this time he can't do any harm. It's after the election—

Perhaps we should save a discussion about Miles for another meeting, Geoff. Miss Harding?

I agree, Mr Braddon. Our friend is not right with the Lord. His heart studies destruction and his lips talk of mischief.

Quite, Miss Harding. So it's agreed then. We'll request these changes, and then we can announce the by-election. And once that's won we can discuss our strategy vis-à-vis Councillor Grayford. Geoff?

I was agreeing with you, John. We get the restructuring through, and then – well, I have plans.

I'm sure you do, Geoff. I'm sure you do.

Denise

At just after six, towards the end of a hot, uncomfortable day, the ventilation in Denise's office had sprung to life. At first she had been grateful, but after half an hour the noise and column of cold air had become painful. Even sitting at her assistant's desk didn't help. The thing clanged with an irregular rhythm, as distracting as the onset of a migraine. She'd gathered up what work she could carry and moved to the Level D canteen, which was cooler than her office, and, at this time of the evening, usually quiet enough for work. Two other senior officers, a man and a woman, were already at other tables. They'd looked up from their files and nodded at her when she came in, but didn't attempt to talk. They were both people Denise saw regularly, sometimes in corridors, usually in this canteen. She didn't know their names: it had never been necessary to know them. Denise was careful not to make friends at work: if you were seen to be part of a group you were vulnerable. Alone, you were less likely to be swept out in the next reorganisation.

But even if you avoided other people you couldn't help knowing something about them. Denise knew the

127

woman lived next door to Alan and Margaret. Once, on a summer evening a few years earlier, she had been sitting in their tiny garden when the woman's face had appeared at the top of the wall. 'Could you please try to keep the noise down? It's nearly midnight.' Denise wondered if the woman remembered her; she also wondered if she was the one rumoured to be having an affair with someone from Parks.

The other senior officer was a red-faced man with an empty right sleeve. She had spoken to him exactly twice, both times about a junior clerk's permission level. They had been typically guarded exchanges: he had managed to convey that he distrusted the clerk without making any definite statements, while she had been careful not to ask any direct questions. In the end they were saved from having to make a decision when the man in question was caught in crossfire in a disturbance outside the Pavilion offices. That had been five years earlier. They had not spoken to each other since.

Denise had brought two files to study. One, the Expedited Transcripts for Perry Tunstall, had been delivered that afternoon, along with another note from the councillor. He now wanted to know about not only 'all matter relating to Henderson', but 'all other possible political activity' – and he wanted a reply by the next day, which meant the four hundred closely typed pages of transcript had to be read that night, and, because of the security level of the request, she couldn't delegate it out to the junior officers – even if there had been any left in the office. It was infuriating because Sarah was hosting a dinner that evening – Doug was working a late shift – and Denise wanted to go, if only because there would come a point – it was usually after the third bottle – when Margaret would start making references to Sarah's children being kept at home. Alan, of course, wouldn't stop her, and the others would just look embarrassed. Denise was the only one who could tell her to stop.

The first few pages seemed to be conversations about building supplies. There was no suggestion of illegality, or even any reference to what was being built. A full investigation would probably unearth some irregularities, but then, given the layer upon layer of unrepealed legislation, where, in theory, you needed authorisation to replace a broken window, there was hardly anyone who hadn't broken the law – either by not notifying the council, or by notifying the wrong department, or by not using approved labour. Building regulations were comprehensive and rarely enforced. A charge based on them would be as weak as a charge based on smuggling.

The door swung open with a bang. She looked up and saw Kieran stride in. He was in uniform, and looked clean and alert, which probably meant his shift had just begun. At first he didn't seem to notice her; she hoped he might be looking for someone else. She was too tired for the forced cheeriness with which you were expected to greet friends of friends.

But he saw her, smiled, and came over. 'Denise, they told me you might be here.'

Who, she wondered, had told him? Her office was empty. 'What do you want, Kieran?'

'Mind if I join you?' He sat opposite her, and looked around the room as if he expected to have to describe it later. 'So this is where you come to get some peace and quiet.'

His gaze finally rested on the transcript in front of her. She closed the folder, provoking a grin. Did he think it was boyish charm? There was nothing boyish about Kieran, and probably hadn't been since his conscription at fourteen. 'I'm not on a break, Kieran. I'm very busy.'

'Is this confidential?' He tried to pull the file away from her. She leaned down against it.

'Kieran.'

He grinned again. 'My mistake. I thought we were on the same side here.'

She tried to smile back. 'I'm sorry, but I have to read and summarise this tonight.'

'So it *is* confidential.' He leaned in closer. 'Actually, that's not why I'm here.'

She nodded at the empty counter. 'It's too late for food.'

'No, no, that's not it either. I'm here, Denise, because I hear someone's asked about my file. Or, I should say, I hear someone has asked *you* about my file.'

So he had heard already. She thought: *Who told you?* It was a pointless question. Even she would have left a trail of paperwork. Somebody who knew the requested file number would know somebody else who could find the name on the register. And how many people in Audit had friends or relatives in Parks? Even she had one. That was the problem with Audit: they were obsessed with secrets they couldn't keep. She said, 'A request was received,' lightly, as if it was nothing unusual.

Kieran held his smile. 'Who requested it?'

'I can't tell you that.'

He gave the merest flicker of frustration. 'It's OK, Denise. I understand you have to do this by the book.'

'I don't have a choice, Kieran.'

'Listen, Denise, I would appreciate any help you can give me.'

'I can't help you, Kieran.'

'Only, a request for my file – that's a serious business. In times like these.' He broke off, as if he'd realised persuasion was useless. 'Were you at the memorial service?'

An odd question. 'Of course not.'

'You didn't go? I thought Jack had been invited.'

'I didn't go.' She realised Jack had not said anything about the service. Once he would have told her, if only to complain. 'I don't have the time.'

'So he didn't tell you? I'm not surprised. He must be under a lot of pressure. It just goes to show, doesn't it? In times like these there's just so much going on. Nobody's as secure as they like to think. We all need to stick together.'

'I can't help you.'

He leaned back. 'Come on, Denise. You could at least tell me who asked for my file.'

'I can't tell you anything, Kieran.'

'I don't appreciate this, Denise.'

She stared him down. 'That's tough, Kieran. These are the rules. If somebody with the correct authorisation wants to see a file I review the contents and send it on to them. But nobody can see their own file or be given any information relating to their own file.'

'Oh, come on, Denise. I'm sure you've looked at your own.'

She stared at him. People had the strangest ideas about what was possible. 'We don't work like that.'

'But you must have looked at Jack's.'

'Kieran, even if I had I couldn't tell you.'

He held up a hand. 'I understand, Denise. You can't tell me anything. But I assume this request has come from high up. Am I right?'

'Kieran.'

'So is it a councillor?' He swung forward again, smiling, as if he'd tricked her into an answer. 'Now, which one is it? Is it Grayford? Or Beamish? Or Lamb?'

'I can't tell you anything.'

'Now – Beamish and Lamb, they're Labour, why would they want to know about Parks?' He pretended to think out loud. 'So it must be dear old Councillor Grayford. His lot have plans, don't they? Is it Councillor Grayford, Denise?'

'You know I can't tell you, Kieran.'

'I'm asking you as a friend, Denise. I thought we could avoid all this red tape.'

'You were wrong.' No apologies; nothing that could give him a foothold. 'It's because you're a friend that I'm not going to report this conversation.'

He showed amusement. 'Report it? A simple little chat between friends?'

'A simple little chat about confidential files.'

He drew his feet back under his chair, as if about to stand. 'Then maybe you should. Because I might report our little chat myself. I wouldn't want to commit a breach of protocol.'

'If you like, Kieran.' She felt tired, weighted to her chair. There were four hundred pages of transcripts to read.

'It doesn't matter anyway. I've got other sources. You know, I could talk to Alan. He pretends he doesn't see much of old Uncle Grayford, but he doesn't fool me. And there's always Jack. I hear he has some useful contacts on the old sub-committee.' He stood up, and glanced at the woman at the next table as if about to ask her opinion, then took a step back. 'Are you going to Sarah's tonight?'

'If I get time.'

'It's good Sarah hasn't forgotten her friends. You know, there are times when I worry we could lose touch with each other altogether.'

'Will you be going?'

'Actually, no. I might have to miss it. Work, work, work, even on a Friday night. I'll see you around, Denise.'

'See you.'

'No, no,' he said aloud, his hand extended towards her as if to stop her from saying more. 'You've told me quite enough.'

He left before she could reply. The other officers were bowed over their tables as if they had seen and heard nothing. Denise waited a few seconds before opening the file again. She was too angry to concentrate on the pages in front of her. If she tried to read them straight away she knew she'd take nothing in, and she couldn't afford to make a mistake. She had a reputation to maintain. If she lost her senior status she'd be as vulnerable as any other officer or assistant – more so, with a demotion on her record. The thought of this cleared her head.

The first two hundred pages contained nothing she could use.

Dear Mr Barrow

Re: claim for compensation.

Thank you for your application form and accompanying documents. However, before we can process your application we will require the following documents:

1   A certified copy of your wife's death certificate;

2   The original (not a copy) of your Employee Additional Cover form (EAC1181);

3   Two copies of the Confirmation of Incident (I regret that for technical reasons this department is unable to make copies of documents).

We will also need to see proof of ownership of the vehicle in question. I am also returning the Medical Assessment form, which requires a second signature in the box indicated.

Once we have these forms I am confident we will be able to process your application without further delay.

G. A. Hoskiss

Re: claim for compensation.

Thank you for your prompt reply. First, please allow me to apologise for our error with regard to your wife's death certificate. This had somehow become attached to another file and hence was not included in the documents I originally reviewed. Once again, my apologies for this.

I note that you have sent only one copy of the Confirmation of Incident. Two are required before we can proceed with your application.

I look forward to hearing from you.

G. A. Hoskiss

———

Re: claim for compensation.

Thank you once again for your prompt reply, and for the second copy of the Confirmation of Incident. I acknowledge that we do now possess three copies of this particular form (the copy sent with your original request had unfortunately become attached to another file). Unfortunately we are unable to offer any reimbursement for the costs involved in obtaining these copies. We can, however, return one of the copies if this is any help to you.

I am now able to assess your application and will be writing to you shortly.

G. A. Hoskiss

Re:

I have received your letter re an application for compensation under our EAC scheme. I enclose a copy of the standard claim form for you to complete, with a list of the required supporting documentation.

N. Grayford

———

Re: app.

Thank you for your letter. I note you have not returned the claim form or included any of the required supporting documentation. It will be necessary for you to return this before your application can be processed.

N. Grayford

———

Re: your letter.

Firstly, I was not aware you had already submitted an application to my predecessor. You did not say this on your letter. I have now found your file. I will write to you when I have time.

N. Grayford

Re: letter.

As I informed you in my last I have only just found your file. I have just started in this job and can't be expected to know everything. I am looking into your claim and will let you know when I have made my decision.

NG

———

Re: claim.

I have looked into your claim and my staff tell me we need the following:

1   A certified copy of the death certificate.

2   A properly signed Medical Assessment form.

Until I receive these I will be unable to take any action with your claim.

NG

———

Re: letter.

I notice your letter did not include any of the documents I asked for. You may well have sent them to this department already, but as I can't see them in your file I don't see how this is relevant. If you want me to do anything about your claim you will have to send them again.

NG

Re:

I see you have written to my department chief. Do you think this is going to help? Your claim has now moved to the bottom of my in tray and I will deal with it in my own good time, and then only when you've sent me the documents I asked for.

NG

————

Re:

I am the senior claims officer, not a filing clerk. As I have already told you, I can't find any of the documents you claim to have sent and sending me copies of my predecessor's letters is not good enough. Just because he said he had received them doesn't mean I can proceed. As for your suggestion that they may have been misfiled, they may have been, but as it isn't my job to find them I don't see what this has to do with your claim. As for your complaint that you can't afford the hospital bills, this is very tragic, I'm sure, but, once again, what does it have to do with me?

NG

————

Re: unauthorised visit to this office.

My staff tell me you called at the office demanding to speak to me. I am not prepared to put up with this kind of attitude. It is unacceptable of you to ask my staff to become involved in your petty vendettas. No doubt you're still congratulating yourself for having 'found', as you call it, the documents in our files. Don't think this will help your case. Whether or not your claim is processed depends on me, and so far everything you've done has only made matters worse. I would also advise you not to waste time writing to anyone else. I am the senior claims officer: my opinion is the only one that matters.

———

Re: letter.

Just who do you think you are? It is bad enough you write to me every day, without repeating lies about me. For your information I was not 'kicked out of Finance'. The move was entirely voluntary, and questioning my competence isn't helping your case. And as for showing my letters to your colleagues, whoever they might be, that won't help you. Your file is at the bottom of the pile on my desk and that's where it's going to stay until you start showing me some respect. I do not want you to write to me again. I do not want you coming to my office again.

NG

———

Re:

Why are you still writing to me? Can't you read? Don't you understand you're wasting your time? I don't care about your application or your hospital bills. I don't care if you have 'friends in the press'. Nobody believes what they read in the papers, especially *The Report*. Which, I would remind you, is unlicensed.

NG

———

Re: claim for compensation.

Please allow me to apologise for my colleague's less than helpful approach to your case. I am sorry you have been put to such trouble in order to resolve what should have been a simple claim, especially in such personally distressing circumstances. I have now taken personal charge of your claim. On reviewing your file I notice that we seem to be missing the following documents:

Margaret

Margaret was proud of the speed with which she processed
clients. She could ask the prescribed questions and announce
a decision in seven minutes, sometimes less. It wasn't
difficult: she had usually decided the outcome after the first
few seconds, based on her clients' expressions and how
they were dressed. In a system that trusted her judgement
she would have dispensed with interviews altogether. In
most cases a half-page report gave her all the information
she needed. 'Isn't that superficial?' Louise would ask.
Margaret thought Louise, whose own interviews were
rarely less than half an hour, was sentimental – always
trying to find out what her clients wanted, as if that could
have any bearing; always, in Margaret's view, looking for
excuses. She would explain that the superficial details
told you everything you needed to know. 'What people
wear – how they speak – that's all there is.' She made
decisions quickly and never had second thoughts. Her
reports were brief and forceful, and sometimes used as
models by the younger workers. That day she'd processed
eight clients held at the Lewes compound. They had been

easy decisions: so easy, she'd finished twenty minutes earlier than even she had planned. She'd left the office with a sense of a job well done and found her driver wasn't in the car park. She had been standing by the empty space, furious that he'd taken on another job (he should have waited, he was *officially assigned* to her), when Jack had driven past, seen her and reversed. He'd just finished a meeting of his own and offered to take her back to the main office. Normally she would have refused: she was supposed to have her own driver. If she wasn't there when he turned up she would feel as if she was letting him off the hook. But she couldn't be sure he would turn up, and that evening she was supposed to be going to Sarah's, and before that she had to get back to the main office and write up the reports. She couldn't afford *not* to accept Jack's offer.

Jack was in his usual bad mood. She told him about her driver and knew he wasn't really listening. As soon as she finished he started complaining about the road. 'This stretch is fine,' he conceded, when she pointed out the way ahead was clear. 'It's when we get to town …'

She asked why he didn't do something about it. 'After all, it's your department.'

'We can't do things just because they suit us.'

'I know. I heard the tape.'

She could have sworn he tightened his grip on the wheel. 'What tape?'

'Of the meeting. After the accident.'

'Oh, that one.' For a split second he took his eyes off the road. 'How?'

She told him about Alan's copy.

'And he took it out of the office?' Jack seemed to

realise he had almost shouted and lowered his voice. 'That's inappropriate behaviour.'

'Don't worry, we destroyed it. It's not as if we passed it on.'

'Alan shouldn't have let you hear it.'

'I do think I can be trusted.' She tried not to sound aggrieved. Strictly speaking, Jack was right: Alan should never have brought the tape home. But Jack should have credited her with some discretion. He wasn't talking to someone like Louise ... 'Do you know where it came from?'

'Have you talked to anyone about it?'

'So far only Alan. And now you.'

'You haven't said anything to your clients?'

'No.' She recognised an opportunity to take offence. Who did Jack think he was talking to? Magnanimously, she let it pass. 'And strangely, they haven't asked.'

'It was irresponsible.'

'The tape's all over the council, Jack. If Alan hadn't played it to me, someone else would have.'

Jack made a noise in his throat. Was he actually growling? 'You shouldn't have heard it from Alan, of all people. My God, what if Tim hears it? It'll be all over Amex.'

'How would Tim know? It's not as if I'd tell Louise.'

'*You* might not.' For some reason the name only made him worse. 'I don't know why she's married to Tim. What's the point of the man? And it's not real, you know, the tape. It's a joke.'

'If it's a joke, what's the problem? Besides, Alan thinks it's real.'

He growled again. 'Alan is irresponsible. He has no regard for protocol.'

'That's not true. Alan has more regard for protocol than' – she prepared a barb, then decided not to use it – 'anyone I know.'

'Of course it's a fake. It's a bunch of comedians trying to make us look ridiculous. I mean, do you really think our councillors are such clowns? That's the kind of attitude that got us where we are today.'

'Where we are today?' Margaret was surprised. 'What are you talking about? What's wrong with where we are today?'

He glared at the road ahead, which was still empty. 'I mean we make a joke of the people in authority and when somebody produces a hoax like that tape people start taking it seriously. And then you get rags like *The Report* writing about it, and that has the potential to cause real trouble.'

'Come on, Jack. Nobody believes *The Report*.'

'But they read it.'

'People like Louise might read it. But they don't necessarily believe it. Though I heard they said the tape was a fake.'

'Did they? That's not the point. It doesn't matter if they're right about this or wrong about something else. It doesn't matter if people don't believe them. They're corrosive.'

'You don't have to tell me, Jack. Alan won't allow it in the house.'

'And Louise reads it? I would have expected her to know better.' There wasn't the faintest trace of a smile. 'Then you know it's important that that kind of rubbish isn't spread. I mean, do we really want people to think our councillors can actually sit down and have that kind of idiotic conversation?'

'Of course not. But, Jack—'

Jack gave a little whinny of contempt. 'And taping it? That's the thing. Taping it. Now if it had been a memorandum ...' He swore. 'Look at this. Traffic. At this time ...' There was a line of cars ahead of them, not moving. Whatever had caused them to stop was round the next bend. Probably just a breakdown, she thought. Some of the cars people drove were barely roadworthy. A twenty-year-old car could break down no matter how carefully it was patched. 'Typical. Councillor Goss all over again.'

'That must have been terrible.'

He nodded, grimly. 'It was. We had to close the road. We lost a day's revenue.'

'I was talking about the accident itself, Jack.'

'Oh, that. It's not the accident, it's the consequences.' He was craning his neck as if to see over the roofs of the cars ahead of them. There was nothing to be seen. 'Councillors come and go. Besides, I didn't see the actual crash. We missed it by seconds. Denise was quite shaken up,' he added, as if his wife's suffering made him more human, though it was hard to imagine Denise being shaken by anything. 'Come on, what's happening here?'

'Is it another toll?'

'It's not one we've authorised.' He said it through clenched teeth. 'They can't do something like this without my say-so. This is just a stupid accident. Some Scoomer in a car that's fallen apart. Or they've been playing chicken.'

'That's what they say about Councillor Goss.'

'That is not what happened.' He glared at her. 'I'm surprised to hear you say that.' Sighing, he let go of the steering wheel and switched off the engine. 'The matter has been officially settled. Repeating that kind of discredited speculation is the sort of behaviour I expect from juniors, not ...'

The line suddenly started to move. Before Jack could restart the engine, the car behind them had overtaken and eased into the newly created space.

Jack struck the steering wheel with both hands. 'The idiot! What does he think he'll achieve by that? Typical!'

'Getting angry isn't going to help.'

'What, and treating everything as a joke is?'

'It'll help your blood pressure.'

'My blood pressure is fine.'

'Besides, who treats everything as a joke? I don't.'

'Not you. I was thinking of Louise.'

'That's Louise.' She wondered why Jack would be thinking about Louise. Had Denise heard something through Audit? Was she under some kind of investigation? Margaret hoped not. Louise was careless and occasionally stubborn, but she was hardly a threat to the social order. You only had to look at the state of her kitchen to see that.

Jack growled, or muttered. The line began to move again, stopping when they had inched the length of a car. They still hadn't reached the bend, so couldn't tell how far ahead of them the line stretched. 'Come on,' Jack crooned. 'If I find out this is because of someone in T and E ...' He sounded as if he hoped it was.

'They'll tell you they're only following orders.'

'And then I'm going to ask who gave them their orders. I have some authority, you know. I'm still the assistant bloody director.' Jack, she thought, was not really speaking to her now, or he was speaking to her as if she was a voice in his head. He stared at the car ahead of them, a clean but ancient Triumph with no rear window, as if trying to move it by the force of his will. 'If everything else in this town turns to shit at least it won't be because of T and E. The councillors can play politics. They can collect their taxes and conduct their little boundary wars and fill departments with their bloody useless nephews. But in T and E, as long as I'm there, we're still going to work to some idea of public service. Even if nobody thanks us for it, even if it does mean sixty, seventy-hour weeks. Unpaid, of course. Even if it means having to argue against one lunatic proposal after another. And if we lose the argument we enact the policy while trying to do as little damage as possible, forever clearing up a mess we didn't make, apologising for mistakes we knew would be made, and covering the arses of people who should never have been employed in the first place. And for crying out loud, what's happening now ...'

They had moved forward the length of another two cars, which had finally taken them round the bend, revealing the obstacle to be, after all, only five cars ahead of them. It was a car parked across the middle of the road, an impromptu barrier, against which two uniformed men leaned casually, as if waiting to start work. Two more uniformed men stood at the roadside, apparently stopping and examining every car.

'A checkpoint,' Margaret said. 'Why have they put a checkpoint here?'

'For Christ's sake, they're Parks.' Jack found a new pitch of indignation. Margaret was amazed at how he managed to find so much variety in such a narrow range of emotions. 'What the hell are they doing stopping traffic? This isn't their jurisdiction.'

'So send a memo.' So much energy expended on things he couldn't change. It was amazing he had any left for work. 'Only five more cars and we're gone.'

'That's right, treat it as a joke.'

'That's because this is a joke.' You didn't have to spend very long with Jack to know why Denise was so sombre. Jack's bile could be amusing at a dinner table, because occasionally he would stop to eat. When he didn't shut up it became exhausting. Margaret liked to think she didn't get angry about things she couldn't control. 'And Parks isn't your department. Honestly, what can you do?'

'My job. The way they should be doing theirs. And no, I'm not just going to sit back and let this happen. Because it's not a joke. When you treat public life as a joke you end up with a choice of clowns. When you don't expect decent behaviour from the people in charge, well then you're just giving them a licence to behave badly.'

'Do you really want to make trouble now?' Somehow his anger had a calming effect. Margaret felt determined to rise above her own irritation. They moved forward another space. 'Ten more minutes and we'll be gone. Start arguing and we could be here for another half-hour. I've got work to do, remember.'

There was shouting from the head of the queue. A driver had climbed out of his car and was arguing with one of the uniformed men. The other Parks man stood behind him, looking out at the line of cars as if he hadn't noticed the argument taking place a few feet away. The two leaning against the parked car laughed, as if at a joke. Margaret was certain they were laughing at the angry driver, a man in his forties dressed in a grey T-shirt and shabby jeans. Unemployed, Margaret thought, or a small-time trader or smugglers' runner. What could he have to argue about? Surely someone like that should know better than to draw attention to himself? Or was he the reason for the roadblock? If he was, why didn't they just take him away? Incompetence on all sides. It was maddening.

'Come on, you bloody idiot,' Jack muttered. 'Don't argue with the idiots.' But the man went on shouting. He waved his hands at the car, at the road, at the other cars. The man he was shouting at occasionally shouted something back – it sounded like the same word each time. Margaret couldn't hear what either of them was saying. A dog in one of the other cars started barking. A pig peered out of the missing back window of the car in front of them, then dropped out of view.

'There's always one bloody troublemaker,' Jack said.

'I thought you were going to make some trouble yourself.'

'Not with a queue of cars behind me.'

The man ahead of them gave up arguing. He climbed back into his car, shaking his head theatrically. His car was waved around the makeshift barrier, and the line moved forward another place.

'Thank heaven for that.' Jack didn't sound particularly relieved. 'For a moment there I thought things could get nasty.' Margaret wondered if he'd been looking forward to things getting nasty. It would have been more fuel for his sense of permanent outrage. 'These Parks and Libraries clowns ...' He trailed off, as the next car was waved through with no more than a glance. 'Clearly one of their friends. Or maybe they're just getting bored.'

Eventually they reached the front of the line. The uniformed man leaned down to their window. He was in his forties, sandy-haired, generically familiar, the way uniformed men of his age seemed to be. He nodded at Margaret, looked for a moment longer at Jack, then at his clipboard, then at Jack again. When he spoke his voice was flat and official. 'Step out of the car, sir.' Margaret winced in anticipation of Jack's response, but he managed to sound surprisingly cordial.

'Can I ask why?'

The man's expression didn't change. 'Step out of the car, sir.'

'I will.' Jack picked up his council ID from the dashboard. 'I was just curious what Parks and Libraries are doing outside their jurisdiction.' He had one hand on the door handle.

The man said: 'Don't waste my time, sir.'

'Of course not.' Jack opened the door, but only slightly. His voice was level. 'As long as you can answer my questions.' He climbed out of the car before the man could say anything else. 'Now what is this about?'

The man seemed taken aback by Jack's assurance. Margaret almost felt sorry for him. He had no idea who he was dealing with. Coming from Parks, he probably didn't realise the significance of Jack's ID. As she watched the man lead Jack over to his colleagues standing by the car parked across the road her only thought was: *You are going to be in so much trouble.*

Your columnist has heard some interesting rumours anent the stout yeomanry of our Parks and Libraries service. It seems that, quite apart from forming unofficial liaisons with the usually shadowy figures of Audit, some of their number have been holding clandestine meetings with the Louis Napoleon of Kemptown, Mr Francis Anthony Henderson, long a favourite in these pages. Your columnist is old enough to remember when the Libraries service had something to do with books. If only they had worked with the St James Street firebrand back then! Who knows, they might have taught some of his followers to read. Pleasantries aside, this new entanglement strikes your columnist as odd. Are they merely working for personal gain, or is it some deeper plot? Much as it is against this citizen's inclination to snitch, if it is merely a matter of personal gain, it is surely not a development the council can afford to ignore, even if it has forsworn such outdated concepts as 'public service' and 'conflict of interest'. Public service! Readers, merely typing the words has left your columnist tearful with nostalgia.

Your columnist's question about two-year-old building permission notices in St James Street was of course a joke. The building work regarding which permission has been applied for but not yet granted is the windowless monstrosity known as the Kemptown Workers' Centre, behind whose reinforced walls Mr Peregrine Tunstall operates his well known import/export business, and in whose capacious lower floor, sometimes referred to as 'Henderson's

Cellar', our town's own Louis Napoleon entertains his followers with imported spirits and his own lachrymose renditions of ancient torch songs. Yes, readers, permission was never granted yet the building was completed without interruption. In fact, some of those 'permission applied for' notices are now attached to the very building for which permission had been applied. Dear readers, your columnist will not insult you by drawing any moral from these circumstances; he will merely point out the salient facts and allow you to reach your own conclusions.

Your columnist would like to make it clear that his earlier allusion to a relationship between certain employees of our Ruling Body was not intended to imply any moral disapproval. After all, even if this affair is conducted at public expense during their usual hours of employment we have the consolation that the happy couple is doing less damage than if they fulfilled their official duties to the letter. No, your columnist is more concerned with the relationship between the firebrand and our favourite councillor. Are our Paolo and Francesca acting as go-betweens, and, if so, why? And does this murky activity have anything to do with the 'accidental' death of our favourite councillor's old colleague and rival? Your columnist does not pretend to know yet, but he will continue to listen.

Bystander

Louise

Tim was up to something. She could tell from the way he said: 'And how was Denise?'

'Denise?' Louise was puzzled. Tim had never shown concern for Denise. Usually he claimed to be scared of her. 'Exhausted.'

'Did she mention me?'

'Should she?'

'I've had some dealings with her at work.' They were driving around the covered car park beside the central market. Tim, as ever, was trying to find a space near a working electric light, a consideration that always added ten minutes to their monthly trip. 'I wondered if she'd mentioned it.'

'She didn't. She was exhausted. She'd been working till ten. You should have been there.'

'Couldn't. I was working. Till eleven.'

'Well, you missed a good evening. Margaret was late and Alan was quieter than usual.'

'I'd have liked to go,' Tim said, automatically. 'We don't see enough of Sarah. How was Jack?'

'He wasn't there. Denise thought he was still at work.'

'Thought he was? Do they even talk to each other?'

'Apparently not. She hadn't heard from him. And apparently didn't ask.'

'So how did she get there? She can't have walked.'

'A driver. She has a driver, you know. And Doug drove her home when he came back.'

'I'm not surprised Jack wasn't there.' Tim glanced at her. 'If he knew you were going to be. He makes a grand declaration and you laugh at him. It would have been too embarrassing for him. No wonder he pretended to be at work.'

'I didn't laugh at him. And it wasn't a grand declaration. And he probably really was at work. You know what he's like. Margaret thought he was giving hell to Parks and Libraries. You know they stopped him at a checkpoint? That's why Margaret was late. She had to drive his car back herself.'

'And then she explained how this meant things are getting better.' Tim shook his head. 'But seriously, they stopped him? I wouldn't want to be in their shoes. The man has a temper.'

'That's why I didn't laugh at him.'

'You laughed when it was me.'

'Different thing altogether.'

'Poor old Jack. It must have been hard for him.'

'It wasn't easy for me. What am I supposed to say to Denise? Every time I see her it's all I can think about.'

'It must have been hard for him.' Tim was preoccupied, and with more than her reaction to Jack or finding a parking space. He was definitely up to something. 'Weren't you even a little bit flattered?'

'I don't know. Do you suppose he thinks I'm a younger version of Denise?'

He almost grinned. 'Surely he couldn't. Mind you, what was Denise like when she was younger? Wasn't she part of a hard-drinking crowd?'

'Doesn't mean she was ever fun. No, Denise was always serious. That's why she married Jack. Somebody to be serious with. I thought they suited each other.'

'Apparently not. You know, I always thought it would be Alan.' He'd found a good space: directly underneath an unbroken light and not far from the door. 'Or Kieran. Or even Doug. Or a client. Or someone I've never met. But Jack?'

'Shows how observant you are.'

He thought about this, or whatever he'd been thinking about earlier. As they passed the guards at the entrance she said, 'What are you planning?'

He smiled ruefully. 'Am I so obvious?'

'Absolutely transparent.'

They walked into the main hall of the market. It was busy but not crowded: there were dozens of people rather than the hundreds you sometimes found when rumours of shortage or abundance swept through the town. On those days the market would be packed tight with people and the security guards could panic and lose control. Louise didn't know how the rumours started: the first she knew about them would be when she arrived at the market and found T & E driving people back with batons. That day the knot of people by the empty shelves in the bread section was still good-humoured and orderly. It was likely they hadn't been waiting more than an hour. Tim said, 'I've been thinking about leaving.'

'Leaving Amex?'

'There's a chance I might be able to work in Canada.'

'Do you think it's any better in Canada?'

'In some places. Where I'd be going.' He corrected: '*We* would be going.'

'I'd prefer Germany.'

'I don't have the choice.'

Louise hated the central market at the best of times. They would set aside a Saturday morning each month, buy whatever they needed as quickly as possible and leave. There were always other places: Scoomer allotments, the guarded farms to the east. Louise knew how to find food. It was easy – as long as you had a reliable car, travelled by daylight, and kept to known roads. They had half a sack of potatoes under the stairs, along with two dozen bottles of wine from Alan's contact, smoked cheeses and cooked meats. It was possible to live well, even here. She thought of their house, the kitchen with her casework spread across the table, their washing drying on a wooden rack, and the smell of bread baking. 'We'd have to give up a lot.'

'I know.'

'Our friends.'

In the next aisle Tim loaded sacks of flour on to the wooden trolley. 'I'd sooner leave. Especially after that business with Goss.'

She said, 'But it was just an accident.'

It was a discussion they'd already had. Tim thought it had been deliberate. The incident nagged at him like a toothache. He was starting to see conspiracies everywhere. He looked around now, as if to see if anyone was listening. The aisle was deserted. 'It was a sign.'

'A sign. You're talking like a Helmstoner.' In the next aisle they found four bags of sugar. Louise loaded two of them on to the trolley. 'Is that the only reason you want to leave?'

'I've been thinking about this for a while.'

'And you didn't tell me.'

'It's only recently there's been a real chance of going anywhere.'

'You've already applied for this job, haven't you?'

'I was going to let you know before I accepted. But it's gone through faster than I expected.' He shrugged.

She faced him. 'They've already offered you the job, haven't they?'

'Not exactly offered. But it's there if I want it.' Again he corrected himself: 'If *you* want it.'

'When exactly were you planning to tell me?' She wished she could have sounded angrier. Even now, she could only sound amused, one step away from indulgent. 'The morning of the flight?'

'Before then.' There was the slightest flicker of a smile. 'We'd have needed a couple of days to pack.'

'Where is it? This job.'

'Toronto. It's supposed to be a good area.' He looked – sheepish? Contrite? Mildly uncomfortable? Nothing so distinct. 'It's not for another month.'

'When do they need to know?'

'By the end of next week.'

She made an attempt at anger. 'And you didn't think to tell me that until now?' It didn't work: she couldn't be angry with Tim, even over something like this. It was a weakness. 'At least it'll give us something to talk about over the weekend.'

He looked relieved: a provisional relief, as if the worst might be still to come. Good, she thought. Let him think that.

They found rice and coffee and two dozen eggs and joined the lines at the tills where they queued in silence. Louise nodded at the security guard who walked up and down their line, truncheon in hand. The man had once worked for Welfare and accompanied her on house calls. What was his name? But he ignored her, which somehow made her angrier than anything Tim had said.

Back in the car park she told him about the guard. 'I used to talk to him all the time.'

'It's his job.' Tim unloaded the trolley into the back of the car. 'Something happens when people put on a uniform.' He looked around the car park, as if he thought someone might be listening. 'Even at Amex. The most harmless men you could imagine. Put them in security gear and they'd shoot you in a heartbeat.' She wondered if he was thinking of a particular person. 'They'd feel sorry afterwards – sorry for what you made them do. But not guilty.'

'Not everybody, surely.'

'Oh, not everybody. But most people. Enough people.' Tim seemed lost in thought again. He didn't say anything till they were out of the car park. 'There's something else you should know.'

'What, that you've already accepted the job?'

A rueful smile. 'Not that. If we do go, Siobhan will be coming as well.'

'Wouldn't Kieran have trouble getting a visa?'

'He wouldn't be going. He's why she wants to go.'

'Kieran?'

'Exactly.' Tim sounded suddenly vehement. 'Everybody thinks they're such a close couple but it's not like that at all. *He's* not like that at all. The only reason they're still together is because she's too frightened of him to leave.'

Her first impulse was to laugh, but his tone was too serious. Tim wouldn't talk like that unless, at the very least, he believed it was true. 'If she's scared of him, how will she tell him she's leaving?'

'She won't. She'll just go. If she told him, she's certain he'd stop her. Kieran's not the person we think he is.'

'How do you know?'

'We talk. At work. It's the only place where she feels safe.'

'And she's told you this?'

'She's told me enough.'

There were crowds on the streets. A rally was planned for the afternoon: Labour protesting against Conservative corruption. Next week there would be a Conservative protest against Labour corruption, then both sides would hold rallies on the same day and the streets would be closed. Louise watched the crowds coldly. They seemed cheerful now, but the mood could change quickly. All it would take would be for one of them to step in front of a moving car, or for the weather to change. Most of the men carried sticks and homemade weapons. Only a few of them seemed to have guns.

She said, 'It's a lot to take in.'

'But it's not unusual, is it?' Tim was also watching the crowd. 'The nice guy, popular with everyone, who's different at home. You must have seen it.'

'Among clients. The pub hero who goes home and beats up his wife ...' It was plausible: Kieran wasn't like them, however much he'd tried to fit in. He was an outsider, of whom anything could be believed. Alan and Jack used to tease him about his potential for violence; Kieran would grin and protest weakly, basking, she now realised, in their implied admiration. 'When did Siobhan tell you this?'

'I'd thought something was up for months. I asked her about it – it was just after the Goss thing.' They slowed as they approached the security gate at the foot of Southover Street. 'There's more as well.'

'Yeah? Who else is coming?'

The gate swung open. Tim smiled at the security guard, an uncharacteristically open smile, as if, later on, they might meet over a beer. 'It's about Kieran. I asked Denise about his file.'

'What did she tell you?'

'Nothing.'

'That sounds like Denise.'

'Oh, I knew she wouldn't tell me anything.'

'So why ask?'

'You know how Audit works. Information comes in, they put it in a file. Nobody reads it or asks what it means, it's filed and forgotten. They never look at anything until somebody gives them a push.'

'So you gave them a push.'

'I just wanted *her* to see it. If there's anything there the council can take care of it.' He turned into their street and parked neatly outside their house. He stopped the engine and faced her. She couldn't read his expression. Of course: that was why Siobhan had confided in him. If nothing else, Tim could keep a secret.

'What do you expect her to find?'

'About a year ago, dollar bills from our vault started turning up in other parts of the county. We looked into it and found the Greaveses were involved.'

'I've heard of them.'

'Amex have been interested in them for a while. We know the routes they use. They're right through Kieran's patch.'

'I've had clients who worked for them. You think Kieran's involved?'

'We made sure the information we had found its way to Audit.'

'So you put it in Kieran's file and then told Denise to look at it?'

'Kieran is dangerous.'

At another time she would have laughed. She couldn't, as if her joke reflex, that usually reliable machine, had ceased to function. Tim wasn't frightened of phantoms. If he rarely said what he did mean, he never said anything he didn't. And Siobhan had trusted him when she didn't trust her closest friends. She said, 'You should have thought of that before you started pushing.'

'I couldn't do anything until I was certain we wouldn't have to stay.'

'No.' She looked out at the familiar street, the old cars and dirty house fronts, and tried to imagine Toronto. She couldn't. 'We'd better go inside. People will think we're arguing.'

From: Cllr Braddon

To: Cllr Grayford

In strictest confidence.

I need hardly tell you how disappointed I was by your nephew's handling of the Barrow compensation matter. I attach the relevant correspondence. Read it and weep, as they say. I thought he wouldn't be able to do any damage in Personnel, but I sadly underrated him. His deliberately antagonistic approach came very close to forcing Mr Barrow to go public with his complaints. I would remind you that it was only my intervention that prevented him from speaking out at the time the earlier false reports were allowed to circulate. Mr Barrow may be a difficult individual, but he does have a legitimate grievance, and some allowance needs to be made for his occasional displays of temper. Your relative, by contrast, has no excuse, and there are only so many ex-gratia payments I can make before Finance starts asking awkward questions (and you know how hostile GP has been to making any payments at all). Your relative proved himself fundamentally unsuited to Personnel and I stand by my earlier conviction that a few months in Parks and Libraries would be good for his character – as long as he was prevented from having any real authority. His tactlessness and inability to work with anyone would have made him an ideal candidate for Process Management, if only he could pass their – or any – test, and if only he hadn't already antagonised them during his earlier stint at Finance. I appreciate he is not employed by the council to carry out actual work, but as far as possible he should be prevented from causing any damage. If he fails in T & E I would advise you to move him either to Parks and Libraries or, preferably, out of the council altogether. The commission we are planning to send to France on the refugee camp issue would be a good appointment.

You may have heard of the recent incident involving the AD of T & E. While doubtless unfortunate for the individual concerned, it strikes me as good news for the sub-committee. It not only removes one of the more awkward members, it also gives us the opportunity to make significant changes to the department as a whole now, without having to wait for the planned restructuring. In particular, it gives you the opportunity to increase your personal influence *without* making any new appointments. The AD's current assistant is a natural choice to replace the AD while he recovers, and should give us all the direct influence we require. I appreciate this will leave the assistant's old position vacant, but I would try to fill this from within the department. I appreciate your desire to do the best for your family, but, in this case, would urge you at the very least to wait until *after* the by-election.

There may even be further advantages. T & E have requested Audit to negotiate with Parks and Libraries regarding an opportunity to interview the officers concerned. My personal preference would be to close the matter without involving the national police, whose role in this kind of case is little more than an expensive formality. An internal inquiry should establish that the incident was the result of the actions of a rogue element within Parks. As with the Barrow case, the former AD and his dependants can be offered compensation, and the AD himself treated at council expense – up to the amount guaranteed by his contract. Officially, the matter will be closed. Unofficially, the result of the inquiry will give us further scope for making changes to Parks and Libraries.

You are right that the work of the present sub-committee is only a starting point. The restructuring will give us the opportunity to make more ambitious changes across the entire region. Certainly a redrawing of the ward boundaries is long overdue, but that should in turn lead to a redefinition of the very nature of regional democracy. Your idea, for example, of linking the right to vote to employment status will certainly be worth exploring. I know it has been rejected before, but with the likely postponement of next year's national elections and the tensions that is bound to cause, I am certain we can convince the observers that security is more important than the merely symbolic gesture of casting a vote. However, we can look at this idea in more detail once we have secured the Goss by-election.

Siobhan

Alan came into the kitchen with an empty wine bottle as Siobhan was rinsing the plates. 'You don't need to do that,' he said, but mildly, as if he didn't really want her to stop. He added the empty bottle to the collection by the side of the fridge (there seemed to be empty wine bottles on every flat surface) and started fussing around his wine rack.

Siobhan turned back to the sink. It had been a mistake to come here. 'I don't mind. I've nearly finished anyway.' She wanted to delay joining the others in the living room, where the talk was still about what had happened to Jack.

Louise had phoned her earlier: 'In case you haven't heard ...' Jack, she said, had been attacked. Siobhan's first thought had been that someone had questioned his competence. No, Louise had said, it wasn't that kind of attack ... She had sounded less cheerful than usual, which normally would have come as a relief. Margaret had been with him at the time. She had seen him being led away and thought nothing of it. Denise hadn't found out until the next morning ... Alan and Margaret, Louise had added, were still going ahead with their dinner. 'It's clearly not enough to upset their routine. And they expect everybody to come. I think they see not having it as giving in, or something. You know what Magsy's like.' She'd quoted an old remark of Denise's: 'To think that acknowledging reality is a sign of failure is just like Margaret.' Siobhan had said she would go. She couldn't think of an excuse not to.

Louise had talked as if the attack was something that could have happened to any of them, like an accident or a disease. She hadn't mentioned Parks and Libraries. Siobhan didn't hear about their involvement until Alan poured the wine and Margaret told them once again about the roadblock and how she had seen Jack being led away. The others had heard this story the previous week at Sarah's. Now it had a different ending: Jack did not show his badge, reassert order, and give these idiots hell. Instead he was dumped two hours later outside the T & E depot on the Lewes Road, without his badge – which meant he wasn't at first recognised. Margaret told the story grimly. After all, she reminded them, she could easily have been a victim herself. 'Do we know who they were?' Tim had asked. 'Not yet,' Alan had answered. 'They were in Parks uniforms. But that doesn't mean anything.' The official version whenever council men seemed to be involved: they must have been deserters, or criminals in stolen uniforms. Thieves dressed as officials ... For Siobhan it had been as if Kieran had walked into the room. If the men who took Jack had been in Parks uniforms it meant they were Parks; it meant Kieran was involved somewhere. 'Of course,' Alan had been quick to say, 'without any real information it's too early to speculate.' 'Absolutely,' Margaret had added emphatically. Siobhan had felt sick.

Gathering up the empty plates had given her an excuse to leave the room; washing the dishes had given her an excuse not to go back. By the time Alan came through with his empty wine bottle she was beginning to think she was in control of herself again, that she'd become the briskly cheerful person she hoped they thought she was, the prim dispenser of conventional wisdom and household advice. 'It's always best to do these things straight away. They're easier to clean.'

'We normally leave them till the morning.' Alan pulled a bottle from the rack, then replaced it and selected another with an identical label. He seemed happier with his second choice.

'The water was working now.' She thought her voice sounded calm. It was as if someone else was talking, some dull, careful sister who, if her life had been different, she would respect and avoid. She would have liked an excuse to stay longer in the kitchen, alone; but Alan would notice she had washed everything, including some dishes that had already been washed. She looked around for a cloth to dry her hands, which gave her another excuse to avoid looking directly at him. 'You know what it can be like in the mornings.'

'Then we leave it till the evening.'

'When the power usually goes.' She shook her hands over the sink. 'It's getting more unreliable.'

'You can't have everything.' He threw her a towel he'd had bunched under his arm. 'At least we still have power. Hastings, on the other hand …' He shook his head, as if he disagreed with what he'd been about to say. 'It's a shame Kieran couldn't make it.'

It was often said, and they never meant it: they only

said it to please her. Yes, she would agree, it's a shame. 'It's his job.'

'I was hoping to talk to him.'

'He's still tidying up after that rally.'

'I thought there hadn't been any trouble.'

'There wasn't much. But they still have people to process.'

Alan frowned. 'They should leave that to Welfare.'

'You know what Parks are like.'

'It's why they need to change.' Alan looked thoughtful, as if he was wondering whether to send a memorandum. 'I wanted to talk to him about Jack.'

It was as if he had jabbed a nerve. 'Why?'

He seemed surprised at the question. 'To see if he knows anything.'

'I haven't seen him.' He had been out; she didn't expect him back until morning. Normally that would have made this a good day.

'No?' Alan looked down at the bottle. He seemed to be studying the fine print on the label – as if labels could mean anything. 'You know, I envy you sometimes. Not having to deal with all this politics.'

'We don't know if it was politics.' She realised she was wiping her hands long after they were dry. 'Besides, Amex has politics too.'

'But not so much, surely.'

'You'd be surprised.'

'I've been promoted. Assistant Director.'

'Margaret said.'

He smiled at her, as if she hadn't understood what he was saying. 'The director came into my office the day after it happened and said, "Something's happened to Jack, so you're in charge." It was as brutal as that. I didn't want to get the job this way, you know.'

'You were Jack's assistant, weren't you? You were the obvious choice.'

'I'm concerned that's not how it looks.'

She recognised the tone: Alan's usual self-pity in its usual transparent disguise. 'Do you think people will think you got the job because of your family?'

'Well, don't they? I know nobody says anything, but that's what they're thinking.'

'It wasn't what I was thinking.'

'Nobody's saying anything. But if they want to see some real nepotism they should see who's replacing me.'

'Not your cousin.'

'Bloody Nathan. Fresh from his balls-up at Personnel, where he was sent following his balls-up at Finance. They give him a position of responsibility in an important department. And at precisely the time we're finishing a major piece of work. Honestly, I want to send him home on full pay just so he can't do any damage. But this time he wants to work. It's as if he's trying to make amends. So I had to find something he could do. In the end I put him on Road Usage Monitoring. I had him out counting cars.'

She laughed because she thought it was expected of her. 'Shouldn't we be going back to the others?'

He made a dismissive gesture with the wine bottle. 'It's when I have to deal with problems like this that I envy you and Tim. I'd like to work somewhere where influence doesn't matter.'

'It matters. There's just a different kind of influence.' She now wanted to join the others rather than have to deal with Alan's worrying intensity. The more he said he envied her the more she'd think about her own situation. 'But if you mean it you could always apply. There's a waiting list, but I'm sure they'd be interested in someone with your experience.'

'I applied two years ago. I was turned down flat.' Alan never forgot a snub. Even now his voice cracked at the injustice of it. 'Do you know why?'

'There were no places available?'

'It was my name. They didn't want to employ anyone with my connections.'

'They actually said that?'

'Not in so many words. But it was obvious that's what they meant.'

'Oh.' When Alan started talking about his family there was nothing you could say. 'The washing up's done.'

Alan wasn't ready to go. 'That's why I envy you, Siobhan.' There was an edge to his voice that reminded her of Jack: the same note of grievance, of barely suppressed outrage at the whole world. Perhaps it was what happened to some men when they reached a certain age, or an Assistant Directorship. 'There are times when I even envy Kieran. I know his job isn't easy either, but he doesn't seem to have my problems.'

'The other man's grass.'

'People say that, but sometimes it *is* greener. I mean me and Mags – we get along, but the pressure we're both under at the moment – if we seem a little tense, that's the reason. I know we have this reputation for arguing.' This was a surprise: if anything, Margaret and Alan had a reputation for not arguing. Louise even joked about how oppressive this made their dinners: 'You never know when an argument's not going to start. You can practically hear the blood pressure rising.' Alan carried on with the same slurred urgency. 'But what's wrong with that? Everybody argues, don't they? It's only natural we should have the occasional disagreement. It shows we're independently minded. And Margaret is – a strong character. So, yes, we do argue sometimes – though, God knows, not as much as Jack and Denise ...' He stopped, as if noticing what he'd just said. 'I mean, everybody knows they argued, but that doesn't mean they weren't, that it isn't – but you and Kieran, you seem to get on.'

She took a step towards the door. 'Have you seen Denise?'

'Mags has. Do you know what she said? That she couldn't come tonight because she has too much work.'

'That's just like Denise.' She twisted the damp cloth in her hands, and turned away, as if looking for something else to clean. What she had wished for Kieran had happened to Jack. She would have felt guilty even if Parks hadn't been involved. 'It must have been a shock.'

'I've seen Jack.' Alan's voice quavered. 'I visited him at the hospital. There were some issues at work that needed to be resolved, but he was ... asleep.' He sounded as if he thought Jack had let him down. 'I would have appreciated his advice.'

'Louise said nothing was broken?'

'Some ribs, they think. They're doing their best for him. I was impressed by how well they're treating him. The hospital is so much better than it used to be. But the whole business is terrible.' He turned the bottle in his hands as if trying to judge the contents by its weight. 'You try to make things better and then something like this happens. And to somebody like Jack. It gives people the wrong impression.

I've even heard people in my own department saying this had something to do with Councillor Goss – just because Jack happened to see the accident. People see conspiracies everywhere. I just don't understand it.'

She raised a hand. 'Maybe you should save this for upstairs.' She had heard enough.

He blinked. Had he been crying? About to cry? 'I'm sorry. It's just that people blow these things out of proportion. They start thinking it's something that happens all the time. Next thing, they're making plans to leave. I can't understand that attitude. This town has so much potential. I mean, you've never thought of leaving, have you?'

'Kieran was in the army.' She stepped round him to the door. 'He'd have trouble getting in anywhere.'

'I didn't mean leaving the country.' Alan smiled, as if he'd caught her out. 'Mind you, I would like to travel. But I'd want to come back.'

'I thought you'd been to France.'

'That doesn't count. And that's another thing I envy you. Amex can send you to Germany. I'd like to see how different it really is there.'

'And you should see the waiting list for that.' Antiseptic, peaceful Germany. A surprising number of Amex staff seemed to spend their evenings conjugating verbs. You couldn't walk down a corridor without hearing them practise their book-learnt second language. They hoped it would be a way of escape, though most of them would never leave. But if she told Alan how many were desperate to get out he wouldn't believe it, or launch into one of his tirades against people who didn't realise how lucky they were. 'Anyway, I've finished here. We don't want to spend the rest of the evening in the kitchen.' End it here, she thought: before he could say another word about how he envied her. 'If you hold that bottle any longer you'll be serving it at body temperature.'

'Right.' He turned the bottle in his hands once again, then slid it back into the rack and pulled out his first choice. 'Besides, it's too late for the good stuff.'

He followed her through to the living room. The others were still talking about Jack and Denise.

Transcript #10907

Geoff, is that you?

Bloody hell, John, do you know what time it is? It's three in the morning for God's sake.

I know. The meeting's just finished.

[   ]

I know. The point is, Henderson—

What's that noise? Are you recording this?

Of course I am.

Jesus Christ.

Look, Geoff, we've been through this.

Can I say fuck. I just want to say fuck. For the record.

We're being recorded anyway. It helps if you have your own record. We've been through this.

Fuck fuck fuck fuck fuck.

But as I was saying—

Three o'clock in the morning. The fucking morning.

Geoff, I know. Now, the meeting—

Can't this wait another four hours? Make that six.

No, it can't. It's best you hear now. Henderson—

Fuck him.

Henderson has made a number of proposals.

I bet he has.

You ought to know what they are.

Do I need to know at three in the morning? Three in the fucking morning?

175

Because it's not going to be public knowledge until, well, it's probably never going to be publicly acknowledged, but it's useful you know this before the rest of the council.

Labour. Bastards.

Exactly. Now, what—

You're recording this because of Audit, aren't you?

Yes. Because we don't want—

So if they're taping this as well, aren't the others likely to find out anything you're telling me? Just a thought.

Audit have an eight-month backlog. They won't even know about this call until next year. The election will be over by then.

Eight months! How much are we paying those people?

Geoff, the backlog is not entirely an accident. Grayford had a real fight getting the staff numbers down to that level. Labour wanted to expand it, remember? They wanted same day reporting.

Accountability. Bastards.

They had their agenda. Now this meeting—

Does Grayford know about it?

He arranged it, Geoff.

It's three in the morning, John.

We couldn't hold it any earlier. You know what Henderson's like.

Fucking gangster.

Unproven allegations. But he's a showman.

Where'd you meet him?

There's a bar in Kemptown. He has offices there. He was supposed to be there at midnight. Half an hour late. Didn't give any reasons, didn't apologise.

I don't know why you bother. Man's a clown.

He has supporters.

Rabble. I say let Transport sort them out. Or Parks.

He has supporters in Transport.

Rank and file. Replaceable.

Not a good idea to sack them, Geoff. While they work for us we can control them.

Who said anything about sacking the bastards? If they're Transport we'll use Parks. They'd jump at the chance.

Interdepartmental friction I want to avoid. Especially with restructuring on the table.

Now could be the best time. It'll make the restructuring easier. Get rid of the bastard elements now. And it'd save us money.

That's a discussion for another time, Geoff. The important thing here is Henderson's proposal.

What does he want?

He's prepared to make us an offer.

But what does he want?

He's prepared to stay out of the by-election.

Which he doesn't have a chance of winning.

Which he could stop us from winning. It's in our interest that he stays out.

I can think of ways to keep him out.

Without creating a situation, Geoff. We want to avoid provoking disturbances. He's a popular character.

Then how come he's never won an election?

If he stands in the by-election he'll take votes from us.

I thought we're taking care of that with the one-ways.

That should be enough. But this is politics. You can't rely on people behaving rationally. Look, Geoff, Grayford wants this.

Bloody Grayford. What makes you think the old fart's opinion is worth having?

He hasn't been wrong yet.

He's been getting good advice, is all. What does Henderson want?

First he asked for Kemptown.

I hope you told him to fuck off.

Not in so many words, yes. That was just a starting position. We can't hand over a ward like that. He wouldn't get the votes even if we didn't stand against him. People have doubts. They'd sooner vote Labour than see him in.

So what did he want?

A job.

A job? Fine. I'm sure he'll make a great admin assistant.

He was more after a directorship. Parks and Libraries.

No. Absolutely no fucking way.

Think about it, Geoff. If we give him that post—

We'll never get rid of him. No fucking way.

Grayford's in favour of the idea.

Then he's turned fucking senile. No way can I support that clown being put in charge of anything. Especially Parks. He's already got one private army.

No, but think about it, Geoff. He stays out of the election, we win. We're in a stronger position. We appoint Henderson.

Stupidest fucking thing I've ever heard.

No, wait. Remember, once we're in the majority we can push through the restructuring we want. Parks and Libraries is going to disappear. After three months there won't be a job for him any more. We pay him off, he's out. Politically, he'll be finished.

He can do a lot of damage in three months.

No, he won't. Don't you see? Once he's in post he'll be working for us. We won't even give him control of his own budget. He'll be there just long enough for us to say we gave him a chance. By then it should be pretty clear the man isn't fit to hold office. Don't you see? That way we can neutralise him politically and then take the real fight to Labour.

I'm not convinced.

Grayford supports the idea.

Yeah. You've said. I don't like it. We support Henderson, that could lose us votes.

We don't appoint him until after the by-election. There might be a bit of ill-feeling at the time, but we'll get over that. Then we get rid of Parks, and Henderson with it. By the next election Henderson will have been forgotten.

I'm still not convinced.

It's going to happen, Geoff.

Because Grayford wants it to happen?

Largely, yes. He sees this as a step to maintaining a permanent majority. That's why I'm phoning you now.

Oh great. I love to be woken up for a policy shift.

It's just that from now on we lay off Henderson.

You mean we're supposed to be nice to him? Fuck that.

No, not nice. You don't mention him. We don't mention him. When politics is mentioned, the opposition is Labour. Henderson isn't an issue.

And what if somebody asks? What if somebody says I hear your lot have made a deal with the old gangster?

You change the subject. You don't criticise him.

Well, I'm not praising him either.

You won't have to. From now on, as far as we're concerned, Henderson doesn't exist.

I think you're [   ]

Thanks, Geoff. I knew you'd understand.

Louise

Louise reached the security gate for her offices just after seven. Her intention was to collect the files she needed and leave before anybody else arrived, something she did most mornings. That day there was only one guard at the gate, a middle-aged man she hadn't seen before. He frowned at her ID card as if it was the first time he'd seen one like it. When she asked if there was a problem he only muttered and repeatedly consulted a handwritten list as if he thought her name should be on it. Louise kept quiet. It was best to say as little as possible to guards, especially if they were new and didn't appear to know what they were doing. She wondered if he would have to telephone for help (it didn't seem to occur to him to talk to *her*), but eventually he was either satisfied, or embarrassed enough to wave her through. Louise crossed the car park, feeling this had been a bad start to the day. How would he react when he saw her trying to take files out of the building? Perhaps she'd have to make sure she was accompanied by one of the guards who did know her ... She noticed a Parks and Libraries jeep in the space allotted for visitors and immediately thought of Jack.

Kieran climbed out, in full uniform. He waved at her, as if across a much greater distance, grinning broadly. 'Louise, how are you?'

There were four other cars in the car park, one of them a shell resting on its axles, but no other people. The security man at the gate seemed to think Kieran was waving at him and waved back, calling out something Louise didn't catch. Kieran noticed him and laughed once, loudly enough for the guard to hear. To Louise he said: 'Used to work for me. Haven't seen him in ages. Good man.'

Louise glanced back. The guard had turned away and was once again watching the road.

Kieran was still smiling. 'So how are you, Louise?'

'What are you doing here, Kieran?'

'I'd just finished my shift.' He stood between her and the door to her block. 'And I thought, I'll see if I can catch Louise before she starts hers, because I haven't seen old Louise for ages.'

'It's not a good time, Kieran.'

'You can spare a few minutes, can't you?' His tone wasn't as cheery as his words, but that could have been fatigue. 'Just for a chat? I hardly see anyone these days.'

'Only a few minutes, Kieran.'

'I know. It's terrible how little time we seem to have. It's all work, work, work, isn't it? If it wasn't for our little get-togethers we'd all go mad, and I haven't been to as many of those as I should. So, Louise, what's happening?'

'You've heard about Jack.'

'I heard.' He looked and sounded appropriately serious. 'That was something you couldn't miss. Terrible business, so unnecessary. They were wearing Parks uniforms, I hear, my own department. You know, I almost feel responsible. How's Denise taking it?'

'She's taking it well. Considering.' Denise had been – what was the word? Grim? Stoical? Whatever it was, she hadn't shown much emotion. They had driven to her house expecting to find her in tears, or at least noticeably upset. Instead they found her savagely matter-of-fact. Louise had been shocked. Afterwards she had joked that Tim, probably for the first time in his life, had been the most talkative person in the room. 'She says he could be in hospital for weeks.'

'You haven't seen Jack yourself?'

'Not yet.'

'No? You should. I should too. It's a terrible business. Do you know, I spoke to Denise on the day it happened? Purely by chance I happened to have some business of my own. Wasn't that a coincidence? But I hear she's at work again. Do you think that's a good thing?'

'You know Denise.'

'I certainly do. Back at work the next day, I heard. Didn't miss so much as a morning. I suppose it keeps her mind off things, but I can't help wondering if that's a good thing.'

'It's what she wants to do.'

'Exactly, exactly. It's what she wants to do. We've all got to support her in that. Give her what help we can in these difficult times. We all have to help each other. She was going to help me, you know, a little favour, but it's probably not a good time to ask her now. You don't remember if she said anything about me, do you?'

'She didn't mention you.'

'I'm not surprised, I'm not surprised. Has Tim spoken to her, do you know?'

'I don't think so.'

'But he's not the kind of man who talks, is he, Louise? Even if he'd been on the phone to her for hours he wouldn't tell you, would he? My Siobhan's just the same. Lovely girl, but not one for gossip. Won't always tell me what's going on.'

'Do you think something's going on?'

'You know this town, Louise. Isn't something always going on? There's always plots and counterplots. Like this Goss business. Very mysterious.'

'Tell me about it.'

'I wish I could, Louise. But I'm as much in the dark as everybody else. Councillor Goss, poor Jack, who knows what's going on? But you must give my regards to Tim. What's he up to these days? Never can tell with Tim – it's like they say, it's always the quiet ones. It's a shame I can't come to as many of your little dinners as I used to. I feel so out of touch sometimes, and Siobhan, bless her, isn't very good at keeping me up to date. I asked her what you all talked about at your last little get-together and she couldn't remember a thing. If you do get a chance to talk to Denise, tell her she has my deepest, deepest sympathies. What happened to Jack was so unnecessary. Will you do that?'

'Of course.' She noticed, with relief, two people from her office coming in through the gate. One of them waved to her.

Kieran noticed the wave. His smile didn't falter. 'Looks like people are starting to arrive. I'll be on my way. It's been a long night. Tell me, who goes out with you when you're visiting?'

She took a step to her left and started to edge around him. 'I don't do many visits these days.'

'Really? You make some though, don't you? Who's going out with you these days?'

She suspected he already knew the answer. 'Roger Kite.'

He seemed delighted. 'No! Old Kitey? He's an old Parks man. I know him well. You'll be safe with him. He'll keep an eye on you. Well' – a glance around the car park: the people from Welfare were only yards away; the guard was still staring out at the road – 'I shan't keep you any longer. But before I go, Louise, how are you? I've been asking about everybody else and you haven't said a word about yourself. How are you, Louise?'

'I'm OK.'

'Because you don't look your usual cheery self. Everything's OK with you, I hope?'

'It's too early in the morning to be cheerful.'

He laughed almost as loudly as he'd laughed at the guard's remark. It was a laugh, Louise thought, that shouldn't have fooled anybody. He started walking sideways back to his jeep. 'Of course, I'm forgetting that for you it's still early. You still need to get to your office and have that first cup of coffee. Well, I won't keep you any longer. It's been great talking to you.' He paused before climbing in. 'Give my regards to old Kitey. And remember, if you see Denise – tell her you saw me.'

She backed away, nodding. Once through the door she ran to her office.

Transcript #12036

Brothers and sisters in Christ, thank you for that gracious welcome. Now, I would like to talk to you this evening about one of my favourite pieces of scripture. It is not one of the prophetic books, or even one of the Gospels, great as these books are. No, tonight I am not going to talk about the end times or the beautiful teachings of our saviour, but about words that have always been a comfort – yes, a comfort – to me in these difficult times. I speak of the fifty-fifth psalm. Yes, you know it well. Isn't it strange how one little song, written I don't know how long ago, can still have such meaning for us? Strange, yes, and wonderful.

Now, thanks to your support I have been able to take the word of God even to the council chambers. And believe me, there have been many times when that word was needed! Many, many times! Brothers and sisters, I have accepted the gift of that responsibility, and it has not been an easy task. Many times I have recited this psalm, sometimes as a silent prayer, sometimes aloud – yes, aloud – as a rebuke to my fellow councillors in the hope that the Lord would touch their hearts. But it has not been easy. Because of the voice of the enemy, as the psalmist says, because of the oppression of the wicked. And the wicked are not just Labour or the independents, oh no. I tell you there are factions in my own party who hate our covenant. Brothers and sisters, they seek to undermine us with all sorts of treacherous dealings.

Now, Labour is our enemy declared and apparent – there's no mistaking what they're up to! We all remember when they tried to take away our children and turn them from the truth. With the Lord's help, and the support of one of the independents, the Conservatives were able to defeat that outrage. It was the Conservatives who gave the Mission the power it now has, to spread the word of God even unto the most wretched, to Russell Street and the Laine, and I'm told we're even doing quite well in Moulsecoomb. What's that? Oh. Are we? That's a shame. But I think that only goes to show the struggle is not yet over, we still have a long fight ahead of us. And that brings me back to the psalm. For, I tell you, I've often wished I had the wings of a dove and could fly away and find rest, to hasten my escape from the windy storm and the tempest. But we can't do that. No, brothers and sisters, even if I did have a dove's wings I would not abandon you. Rather, with the psalmist, I would call upon the Almighty to destroy our enemies, to divide their tongues, and, above all, to guarantee a continuing Conservative majority. Because only the Conservatives can save you from the snares of Satan and godless Labour. But even among the Conservatives there are some who are not pure of heart, who are blind to the light of God's wisdom.

I know that some of you thought Councillor Goss was one of these. But I am here to tell you to pay no heed to the vicious talk of unbelievers. Now, I know Councillor Goss was not a perfect man. I know he had weaknesses it's perhaps best not to dwell on at this unfortunate time. But his heart was with the Lord, even if he did lack resolve when faced with temptation. We can't all be saints, after all, and, as Christians, we must make some allowances for our weaker brethren.

Where was I? Oh yes. Councillor Goss. Many times he knelt beside me in the council chamber, calling upon God to change the hearts of the wicked. No, he was not our enemy. We know who our enemies are. Like the psalmist, we have seen violence and strife in the city. Day and night they go about it, wickedness is in our midst, and deceit and guile depart not from our streets, and so on. Brothers and sisters, we know this, don't we, because we see it every day.

Where was I? Enemies, yes. For it was not an enemy that reproached me, neither was it he that hated me that did magnify himself against me, but it was – is, I should say – is a man mine equal, my guide, yes, and mine acquaintance. That's what the psalmist says. I think there's a message there. I think you know who I mean, don't you?

We live in perilous times. The end draws nigh. And what does the psalmist say? Let death seize them, and let them go down quick into hell! Quick into hell! That's the fate promised – yes, promised – for our enemies. Such beautiful words! Truly this book – these beautiful words – have been a rock and consolation for me, as I know they have for all of you, even those of you who cannot read them for yourselves. It is the reassurance that God will hear us. Evening and morning and at noon we pray and cry aloud – it's true, isn't it? God will hear, and will afflict our enemies, even the ones who seem to be our friends. You know who I mean. I'm sure he has spies here tonight. Let us pray that the Lord will touch their hearts.

Brothers and sisters, brothers and sisters, the man I mean is described in this very psalm, this fifty-fifth psalm. Isn't that proof of God's wisdom? Doesn't that show that our faith is right? What more proof could you need? For the words of his mouth are smoother than butter. That's what it says, and it's true, as I can vouch for myself. But as the psalm says, war is in his heart. His words are softer than oil, yet they are drawn swords. Yes, his words are drawn swords and there is war in his heart. He may fight alongside us now, he may be an ally now, but we cannot trust him even though he is also a Conservative. And when we have defeated Labour – when God has brought them down to the pit of destruction – then we must make a stand against the ungodly in our own ranks, mustn't we. Yes, that will be our next task. And this man – yes, him, I will not name him! – seeks power on this earth, yes, and power will be given to him for two and forty months, which will have to be after the national election. So that's two years away, unless there's another postponement. Now, those of you who know the book, and, yes, I am not quoting the psalm now, you will know the signs. Two and forty months, that's three and a half years, isn't it? Three and a half years in which he will make war against the saints. Yes, I know some of you thought three and a half years was the length of time Councillor Goss was in office, but if you look at the date he actually took office you'll see it was only thirty-nine months. We must be careful not to misread the signs, the way some of our brethren last year – oh dear, that was so unfortunate. The times are close – you can see that, can't you? But they are not yet upon us. We must avoid the snares of the devil, you know. We must prepare for those times, the times when, as the book says, he that leadeth into captivity shall go into captivity, he that killeth with the sword must – must, brothers and sisters, not may, not ought to but we'll make an exception this time, no, must – must be killed with the sword. These are not my words; these are the teachings of God himself. This is the revelation he gave to John I don't know how many years ago. And every day we see this prophecy coming closer to fulfilment. Isn't that marvellous? So it's God who tells us to do these things, and who are we to say no? I mean, really? So if we're suffering now we know that one day it will come to an end. We know this because God has promised us, hasn't he? As the prophet says, he will make the defenced city a ruin, he will bring down the noise of strangers. Yes, as the heat in a dry place, even the heat with a shadow of a cloud. These are difficult words, I know – difficult, difficult words! But beautiful! And if you read them with the rest of this wonderful book the meaning is plain. He promises a day when there will be no more sorrow, or death, or pain, and we will drink of the fountain of the water of life. Such a beautiful picture, don't you think? How could anybody whose heart had not been hardened by Satan oppose us? I mean, really? But they, you know, the hard-hearted, the branch of the terrible ones, perhaps the strangers, yes, the strangers! They will be cast into the lake of fire. Imagine that, being raised from death and hell only to be cast into the lake of fire, the second death! Wouldn't you feel silly!

Where was I? Thank you, yes. I was talking about the psalms, and how there are many lessons to be drawn from the book, that was where I started. But we always come back to prophecy, don't we? We always come back to the end times that are drawing near. How can we stay silent? But my message tonight is that, whatever your thoughts about some members of the Conservatives – and I am, you know, proud to be a member – it is important you support us in the by-election. They may not be perfect, you know, and one of them is in fact evil, but far better them than Labour, with their godless so-called education. Yes, our task is clear. First we must, with the Lord's help, destroy Labour. The other one – yes, him, whose words are smoother than oil – the Lord will destroy at the appointed time. Until then, I urge you in the name of God the Father to support the Conservatives so that the word of truth can be heard in the counsels of the wicked. And now I think it would be nice if we could pray for the lost souls of Moulsecoomb, and all the other Labour supporters.

Thank you all.

Margaret

Margaret stood by her kitchen sink. 'Everybody says "Poor Jack, poor Denise". And don't think I can't see why. But I was there. I saw it.'

Tim stood by the wine rack, his head bowed. He had called, he said, looking for Alan. 'It must have been terrible.'

'You keep asking yourself: could I have done anything different? Could I have stopped them?'

'You didn't know.' Tim looked down at the floor, as if he expected her to burst into tears and couldn't bear to watch. 'You couldn't have known.'

'But I should have known.' Even now, more than a week later, the thought of what had happened made her angry. 'I should have known something was wrong. The roadblock, there, the way they were stopping cars at that time of the afternoon – it was all wrong.' She hadn't noticed the signs, that was what was so infuriating: not that these things could happen, but that they could take her by surprise. She had blamed her driver. If he had been on time she wouldn't have accepted the lift from Jack. Of course she had made a formal complaint – she would have made one anyway – but he seemed to have disappeared, the way drivers often did. 'And when I saw them leading him away all I could think was they were going to be in trouble.'

'You couldn't have done anything.'

'I know. But that's not the point. I should have seen the signs and told Jack to turn the car round.'

'He wouldn't have done that.'

'I know, but I can't help thinking that if I'd said something he might have realised.'

'Jack's stubborn. If he didn't think anything was wrong not even you could make him turn round.'

The reassurance brought a lump to her throat. She swallowed hard. She was not weak. 'We've got complacent. Even when one of them told me to drive away, all I could think was that they were making a mistake. I almost felt sorry for them. When I took his car back I told Denise what had happened and she thought the same thing: they're out of a job, they don't know who they're dealing with. It wasn't until he was found ...'

He took her hands. 'I know. Terrible.'

It was a few seconds before she could speak. Margaret thought of herself as a clear thinker, but for a moment she couldn't think of anything at all. She even found herself blinking back tears.

Tim held her hands gently. For a moment she was reminded of a Helmstoner she'd once interviewed, the head of one of their missions, a man who claimed to have the gift of healing. He had taken her hands in the same way, gazed into her eyes, and asked in the mournful sing-song the believers cultivated, 'Why do you hate us? What evil is in your soul?' She had warned him that if he didn't let go she would call the guard.

Tim was less calculating. He held her hands as if he'd taken them in a spontaneous gesture and wasn't sure how to let go. She found his presence oddly comforting, like that of an intelligent pet, something that could sense your mood without feeling the need to explain it to you. Louise joked that Tim never told her anything. Margaret began to feel this was something in his favour. Alan, she sometimes felt, would be better for having less to say.

Tim said, 'I can't imagine what it would be like.'

Another contrast to Alan, who had spent what seemed like hours trying to *put himself in her shoes* until she'd started to think his display of sympathy was another form of showing off, like his endless boasting about his work ethic, or his tedious insistence that he wasn't like the rest of his family.

Thinking about Alan didn't exactly cheer her up, but the sudden rush of energy – or scorn – seemed to dispel some of the fog. She felt more like herself again: the capable, forthright person other people looked to for guidance. She was a woman who usually knew what was best for other people, and would have told herself – sharply, but for her own good – to snap out of it, as if anger could be an antidote to grief. She was the one who had seen Jack being led away; people didn't appreciate how difficult that was for her. What if they had led her away as well? Nobody seemed concerned about *that*.

And you had to wonder what Jack had done for this to happen to him. After all, his name had been on a list – perhaps the only name on the list. Something like that wasn't an accident. But you couldn't point this out to people. For now, it was all 'Poor Jack, poor Denise'.

Tim had released her hand. He stood with his back to Alan's wine rack, and picked up the mug of coffee, surely, by now, cold, apparently feeling no compulsion to say anything. It made a pleasant change.

But Alan, for all his faults, was a good man. He deserved to take Jack's place, even if it was something else she couldn't say while everybody was worrying about *poor Jack* and *poor Denise*.

She said: 'It's a shame you missed Alan.'

'It's unusual for him to work weekends.'

'It used to be. He had a call this morning. Something to do with a sub-committee he's on. He's working so much more since he took over from Jack. I tell him that these days he sees more of Doug than he does of me.'

'So Doug's his minder? I haven't seen him for ages.' Tim said what the men in their circle always said about Doug, wistfully, as if he missed seeing him. As if he'd forgotten how awkward it was when Doug was actually there and nobody could think of anything to say while all Doug could talk about was his fights (to the men) or his kids (to the women). 'How is Sarah these days?'

'Busy with the kids.' Which meant exhausted. Margaret could not understand why people had children when there was still so much work to be done. Sarah, she sometimes thought, was immature: she'd had children as a way of avoiding responsibility. Her choice of a husband was irresponsible too, though Doug, surprisingly for someone with his background, was supposed to be good with children; as good as anyone could be, given the hours he worked. He would stay at home and look after them while Sarah visited her old friends; he didn't drink. Margaret was unimpressed by these virtues. 'You know what surprises me? She doesn't want to send them to nursery. At least it would give her a break.'

'A lot of parents don't.'

'Helmstoners. Russell Street types. Sarah's one of us. She's exactly the sort of person who *ought* to send their children.'

'You'd think so. But Louise gets quite a few cases—'

'We're not supposed to talk about the cases.'

Tim was loyal. 'Oh, it's not as if she discusses details.'

'Even so.' Margaret reined herself in. She had been meaning to talk to Louise about the confidential files Alan had noticed on her kitchen table 'where anybody could see them'. Alan had been understandably concerned, though Margaret had been able to talk him out of filing a formal complaint. 'It's Louise. What can you expect?' But something would have to be done – perhaps after the election. 'I've spoken to Sarah in the past, and given her all sorts of reasons, but she's quite adamant about keeping the kids at home. I just don't know what she's got against the nursery system.'

'I pass one on the way to work,' Tim said, as if changing the subject. 'I see them in the playground at early morning drill.'

'It's sweet. But Sarah wants to keep them out of the system. And we can't make her.' Actually, they, meaning the council, could. Whether they would depended on other factors: ties to the council, usually. Contacts. Margaret disapproved.

Tim nodded. 'When are you expecting Alan back?'

'I couldn't say. Really, I've barely seen him the last few days. He works a lot out of the office. That's why he takes Doug with him. You know.'

'After what happened to Jack.'

'Exactly.' It occurred to her Alan had been travelling with Doug for months. Had he known something might happen? Alan was astute, she thought; Jack should have been. What had happened to him was his own fault; what could have happened to her would have been his fault too. 'You can't take chances.'

'I just hope we're not going back to what we were.'

'No,' she said emphatically. 'What happened to Jack was bad, but I'm sure we'll get to the bottom of it. As for going back to the kind of disturbances we had – we've made too much progress. It simply isn't possible.'

'I know, I know,' Tim said, as if he had merely mentioned someone else's opinion. 'But still – it's not a good sign.'

'It's not a sign at all. It's just ...' She didn't know what it was. Not wanting to seem irresolute she said, 'I think what happened with Jack was some kind of mistake. We just need to find whoever is responsible and deal with them appropriately.'

'I wonder if we'll ever know.' Tim gave a faint show of emotion, though she couldn't tell which one. 'What is it Denise says? About rumours passing for facts? There are too many rumours in this town. Like this business with Goss. Jack saw the crash, didn't he?'

This surprised her. 'Why? Do you think there's a connection?'

'No, that's probably just a coincidence. I know there are documents circulating, different versions of the official report. If you can believe any of these things ...' He seemed about to say more, and then stopped himself. 'Have you heard from Kieran lately?'

'Kieran never says anything. Besides, I expect he's been busy recently. There is going to be a by-election, you know. It takes up a lot of resources.'

Tim flinched. 'I just wondered if he knew anything.'

'About Goss? Why should he?'

'About Jack. Kieran's Parks. He might have heard something.'

'The uniforms don't mean anything.' Margaret stiffened. Tim seemed to be showing too much interest in things that didn't concern him. She blamed Louise. 'After all, there are all sorts of elements in Parks. And even if he did know something, he wouldn't tell us.'

'You're right.' He held out his mug, awkwardly, as if searching for somewhere to put it. 'You never know what you can believe. Like that tape about the toll roads.'

'You heard that?' Margaret was – not exactly shocked. Louise must have told him; she might even have played it to him. 'That shouldn't have left the council.'

'Oh, I only read about it. Was it real?'

'Alan thought so.' Jack, she remembered, hadn't. 'Alan should know.'

'*The Report* said it was a fake.'

'You can't trust *The Report*.'

'But if the tape was real, doesn't that make it worse?'

'That's not the point. *The Report* is unlicensed.' It amazed her that somebody as outwardly sensible as Tim … But no: it had to be Louise's fault. She was the kind of person who'd read *The Report* and find it amusing. 'They're a bad influence. Have you seen the things they write about Welfare?' Tim seemed to take a step backwards. Margaret realised she'd sounded angrier than she'd intended. 'It's just they have caused so much trouble for us.'

Tim sighed. 'I suppose Alan would know.'

Margaret took the mug from him. 'He has the family connections.'

'He mentions them occasionally.'

She laughed, despite herself. 'Is there anything you want me to tell him?'

'No. I wanted to see him about the reorganisation. You know, what T and E's position on the stadium would be, once Parks is disbanded.'

'That's not going to happen until after the by-election.'

'If the Conservatives win.'

'In that ward? Of course they'll win.'

He seemed to be about to object, then to think better of it. 'I suppose we'll find out soon enough.'

'I'll tell Alan to call you. I don't know when he'll be back, though. If he's on the road he could be late.'

'Congestion.' He nodded. 'Now, that has been getting worse.'

'I'm sure it's only temporary.'

'Of course.' Again there was a flash of an emotion she couldn't identify. He gave a thin smile. 'Thanks for the coffee.' It was only when he was gone that she wondered how he knew about the plans for Parks. Louise: it had to be Louise. The woman was impossible.

From: Cllr Braddon

To: Cllr Grayford

In strictest confidence.

Firstly, I am pleased to hear that T & E have nearly completed the toll road adjustments. I am also pleased to have heard no bad news regarding a certain relative of yours. I hope this means he is being kept on a very short leash.

Secondly, I understand that Henderson has not yet accepted or rejected our offer. We need to agree on what concessions we are prepared to make in order to secure his cooperation. I have initiated enquiries concerning his associates, although we will not be able to take action against them until the day of the election at the earliest. Until then he needs to be handled carefully. We need an answer from him before the report on the Goss incident is made public.

However, once Henderson is no longer a factor and

the restructuring is complete we will be free to focus on long-term goals. The situation where we control Transport and Environment while Parks and Libraries remains in Labour hands is patently absurd, and the rationalisation sub-committee is to be applauded for finally acknowledging the obvious – it must have cost them quite an effort. However, their proposals do not begin to address the growing problem of cross-party cooperation. If unchecked, this could present a greater threat to our long-term aims than the sporadic armed conflict that characterises our current interdepartmental disagreements.

There is also the issue that the present system gives far too much weight to dubious notions such as 'experience' and 'expertise'. Length of service is too often seen as a recommendation instead of a disadvantage, while the shibboleth of 'expertise' merely allows organised and supposedly non-political units to establish themselves, as happened with Process Management. By reducing the scope for patronage, this kind of thing devalues the importance of the political element.

Audit, unfortunately, are currently untouchable for well understood reasons, and the quasi-autonomy of Process Management is a situation that should never have been allowed to arise. The council was negligent, and made a series of decisions we can now see were short-sighted. The council should have taken the opportunity to shut down the whole department at the time when the original application licences were due for renewal. Instead we accepted their offer to develop their own processes and take on work from other departments, on

the grounds that it would be cheaper in the
long run. All too often these departments traded control
of key functions in return for convenience and efficiency,
with the result that Process Management came to be
seen as essential for the day-to-day running of the
council. We are now unable to remove anyone from the
department
without severe disruption in other areas. If we saved
money it was at the cost of losing political control. Once
the first stage of restructuring is complete we really
should look at removing this growth.

There are similar problems in Welfare. While security
issues ensure a high turnover of case workers, there
are still too many staff who have not fully adapted to
the changing role of Welfare; they still behave as if
they were some sort of advocate for the targeted social
groups. Again, steps should be taken.

I am not, however, proposing immediate action. Once
the election has been resolved we can deal with the
remaining legacy appointees. This will not necessarily
entail the wholesale replacement of known Labour
supporters/appointees. Many, I am sure, could be
persuaded to reconsider their allegiance. This, you will
appreciate, will also contribute to our long-term plan of
making the Conservatives the dominant political force
in the region for the foreseeable future, and, ultimately,
once we recover control of Newhaven harbour and
resolve our differences with the Kent Conservatives,
making Central Sussex once again a force in national
politics. This is only possible if we overcome the political
antagonisms that have divided this region for too long.

And if our recent history has taught us anything it is that there is only one truly effective way of ending dissension.

Siobhan

Eventually the security guard had let her climb the broad staircase to the Miles Grayford Ward. She'd had to invoke Kieran's name, which had filled her with a peculiarly cold fury, as if she'd been forced to tell a lie. At the top of the stairs on the left another security guard stood by the door to the ward; to the right, the next flight of steps led up to darkness. Apart from the guards the building seemed to be empty.

This guard must have overheard her argument with the one at the desk; he stepped aside before she had a chance to say anything. Siobhan was almost disappointed: she was angry and would have liked to berate someone. At the same time she was relieved she wouldn't have to mention her husband's name again. Once through the door she found herself in a narrow corridor lit halfway along its length by a single dull bulb, and then by some fainter light from an open door at the end. She was surprised at how run-down everything seemed. This was supposed to be the no-expense-spared ward for councillors and senior officials, yet it was empty. Not unoccupied: empty. Every room she looked in was bare. There were no beds, or equipment, and there was a stale smell to the air.

Jack was in the room at the very end, the one the light came from. He – at least – had a bed, and sat half upright, propped in place on three pillows with a tube in his arm attached to a drip. The light came from a small bulb on the wall behind the bed. His face was lost in shadow. Siobhan couldn't tell if his eyes were open or closed, but thought she could make out the bruising on the parts of his face she could see. She whispered, 'Jack.' If he was asleep she didn't want to wake him.

She would have preferred him to be asleep. 'Jack, it's Siobhan.'

His head shifted slightly, but he didn't say anything. It occurred to her that he *couldn't* talk. Tim, who had visited him the day before, claimed the staff were vague about the extent of his injuries. If his jaw had been broken, Siobhan thought, there would have been bandages. As far as she could tell there was not as much as a sticking plaster.

'I heard what happened.' His head shifted again. Was it a nod, or was he trying to turn away? 'Can you talk?' This time he didn't move. Siobhan took another step forward, wondering if he had really moved the first time. What she had seen could have been a trick of the light, or the automatic stirrings of someone asleep or unconscious, but still in pain.

She lowered herself carefully on to the edge of the bed and leaned closer. The faint glint of his eyes showed they were open and that he seemed to be looking in her direction. 'Jack, this is terrible. How are you?' There was an exhalation, like a sigh of contempt for such a stupid question. 'I know, I know. You're obviously feeling terrible. At least – at least they're looking after you now.' But were they? Leaving him in this apparently deserted ward looked more like storage than care. 'At least you're not in one of the public wards.' Did he shudder? And was it at the thought of the public wards, or at her crass attempt at consolation? 'My God,' she babbled – it was nerves – 'those places. You go in with a cut and you come out with diphtheria ...' She wondered if she should tell him the scene she'd witnessed at the entrance: the two hysterical women, Russell Street types, carrying between them a man with a bloody stomach wound they swore had been caused by an accident. The man had been silent throughout, except to gasp for breath; a thin, horribly pale man who could have been any age between fifteen and thirty. He was small, but the women had still staggered under his weight. They didn't seem to understand they'd come to the wrong building; they had pleaded and screamed until the guard had struck one of them in the face with his rifle. Siobhan had waited until they were out of sight, their wailing still audible, before she'd dared approach the guard. He'd raised his rifle again and shouted at her to go away. Still shaking from what she'd just seen, she had almost lost heart. But she'd steeled herself and demonstrated she belonged to the official class. She had been determined to see Jack, though she couldn't have said why it was important.

'But this place – it's emptier than I expected. Have you seen the other rooms? No, you probably haven't. They're barren ...' He made a sound, as if he was trying to clear his throat. She waited for him to finish, but he seemed to give up. Seconds passed. He couldn't, or wouldn't, speak. She still had the sense he was looking in her direction. 'I feel responsible,' she said, and was suddenly conscious of someone else listening. She glanced at the door. There was nobody there. She turned back to Jack. 'It may sound ridiculous, but I do.'

He spoke: 'Is.' Or was it 'Ease'?

She realised he meant 'Denise'.

'She's not here now, Jack.'

'Lo. Ease.'

'It's Siobhan, Jack.'

He gasped, as if out of breath. She was reminded of the wounded man slumped in the arms of the hysterical women.

'You don't have to talk, Jack. It's stupid of me to ask. I just came to say how sorry I am about everything. I think this is happening because of me. I don't know why or how and I know it sounds stupid because I can't prove anything and if you pushed me I'd have to say I don't really know what I'm talking about, but I think this is my fault. I know it sounds stupid and maybe it is stupid ...' She paused. She didn't know why she was there or what she was trying to say. That Kieran was responsible for all this? She had no evidence of Kieran's involvement, and no idea why he should be involved. It was just her conviction that whenever anything bad happened he would be implicated somehow. 'I should have told you the truth earlier. But I couldn't. It would have been my word against ...' She glanced at the door again: still no one there. 'I couldn't do it. I know Amex would have done what they could, but even they can only do so much. This isn't their town. If it became too difficult for them they'd fire me without a second thought. So I put up with it. Put up and shut up. And then I go out at night and listen to my friends saying what a great person my husband is. I hear them joking about what he does of an evening and secretly admiring him because he gets his hands dirty while the rest of you sit at desks and argue with other departments and send each other memos. And then Tim realised something was wrong. Tim was the only one to realise something was wrong. He's the one who's not supposed to notice anything, and yet he was the one who saw ... And when I told him there was nothing wrong he didn't just walk away. He wouldn't let me lie about it. Do you know what that means?'

Jack breathed: 'Ease,' which, for a moment, sounded like an appropriate answer.

'I should have told him it wasn't his concern. But you know Tim. You give him a problem and he'll try to find a solution. And I can't help thinking that he's why this is happening. It's all because of my bad judgement.'

His faint voice: 'No.'

'Maybe you're right. But I can't help feeling this is my fault.'

Siobhan paused. She had the sudden conviction there *was* somebody in the corridor; somebody standing very still and listening intently. She couldn't have said how she knew; only that she was conscious of being the object of an attention that wasn't Jack's. 'Just a moment.' She touched Jack's hand as she got up from the bed, as if to reassure him she would be coming back.

The corridor was still empty, the door at the end still closed. She could see the guard – she assumed it was the same one – through the frosted glass panel. Could he have been listening? It seemed unlikely. Security guards didn't eavesdrop. The council employed too many other people to do that.

She listened carefully, trying to distinguish the sound of another person breathing or perhaps shifting on their feet from all the muffled scrapings and cries that seemed to come from every side. The hospital was full of noises: closing doors, footsteps on staircases, the squeak of heavy objects dragged across polished floors. As she listened, the building itself seemed to creak, the way she imagined a timber ship would creak. Beyond that there was the occasional hum of a passing car and the more distant sounds of a rally, a man's voice distorted by loudspeakers, the festive crackle of gunfire.

Once she had reassured herself the rooms were still empty she went back to Jack's bed. He didn't move or make a sound, though, as before, she was certain his eyes were open. He was probably drugged, she realised. Even if he appeared awake – even if he actually *was* awake – there was no certainty he had understood what she said or had even recognised her. But she had known this before coming here; his weakness was the condition on which she came. She wouldn't have said as much to him if he'd been his usual self. She would have fussed over him and looked suitably doleful and not said a word about Tim or Kieran. She would have been *her* usual self.

She wondered if there was a microphone in the room, then why she hadn't thought of this before. It was understood the council tried to record everything. It was possible they'd try to record Jack's visitors as well. At Amex there were jokes about the absurd range of the council's ambitions, and how their ponderous machinery left them with more information than they could handle. It was said there were rooms full of cassettes of phone calls, some of which would be recorded over without ever having been transcribed. Amex employees were warned against using external phones for any kind of business. There was probably a microphone here, in this ward. Siobhan doubted if anyone would be listening, and thought that if they were, they would be listening only to hear if there was a visitor. Then whoever it was would push a button to start the recording, and go back to reading their book or knitting. It would be a young woman, she imagined, sitting at something like a switchboard, monitoring a dozen or so conversations in which she had no interest. It would be a young woman because they were allowed to work in offices. The men, unless they had contacts, were put into uniforms and taught parade drill and a kind of military discipline. The council seeped into every part of the town's life; it told people where they could drive, what they could buy or sell. It listened to their phone calls and taught their children how to march.

'When I came here,' she said, 'I thought it would be different. I thought it would be, I don't know, more relaxed. Because it was once a holiday town. Did you ever hear that? People from London used to come here for holidays. Because of the sea and the piers. Can you imagine it? A holiday town. But it's as bad as anywhere else I've seen. It's just as poor, just as violent. We spend just as much of our time pretending we can't see what it's really like.'

Jack didn't respond. Siobhan wondered what it was like for him, of all people, to be unable to speak. Or perhaps all his anger and strong opinions were only possible because he'd never been harmed, and now the violence that surrounded them had reached out and touched him he didn't have anything to say.

She couldn't know. She had her own anger now.

'We have security gates and we think we're safe. Is it like this everywhere in the world? There'll be an election soon. How many people are going to die in that? And we barely notice them because they live on the wrong side of the wall. We treat them like fodder ...'

Kieran was at the heart of her anger; with his night patrols and grim humour, his blind eye to smugglers, his own deals. Kieran was happy with the town. But he was only part of the reason she wanted to leave. Jack, speechless on his bed, was part of it too; so was everybody else she knew. Denise, compiling her reports, was a part; Louise and Margaret, deciding who could live where, turning over children to the Trusts and Missions and council farms as if they were acting in the public interest, were another. At least with Amex there was no pretence. They knew they worked for money.

'I'm leaving, Jack.' It didn't matter whether he could understand her or not. She wasn't so much talking to him as to the imagined woman at the switchboard, to the town itself. 'The day after the election. I won't even be here to find out who wins.' A border pass to Croydon Aerodrome, a flight to Paris, then another to Canada. Tim had the tickets and visas. 'I won't care any more. I just wanted to let you know how sorry I am that this has happened.'

Jack didn't respond. Drugs, perhaps, or exhaustion; or he didn't care either. She backed out to the corridor. 'Goodbye, Jack.' Then she turned and walked away, head held high, as if she'd been here on official business now successfully concluded. The guard stood to attention as she passed and gave an odd jerk, as if suppressing an impulse to salute. He wasn't hospital security, she noticed, but Transport. An additional guard, because Jack's department didn't trust the other departments. Yet another reason she would be glad to leave.

Transcript #21368

Frank? Is that you?

[   ]

What? Listen, can you hear me?

[   ]

Worried? No, I can hear you. You sound terrible. Yes. I said terrible.

[   ]

Car phone, right. Are you sure that's safe?

[   ]

I said safe. Safe. We've talked about this.

[   ]

The report? What report?

[   ]

Oh, that. Well don't read it then. You don't expect them to like you, do you?

[   ]

Well you shouldn't. They're never going to like you.

[   ]

Because it's paid for by Amex. Everybody knows that. They don't like the council and they don't like you and there's no point worrying about it. They're never going to like you. Don't tell me this is what you wanted to talk about.

[   ]

Did they. We shouldn't. No. We shouldn't.

[   ]

What? Because they're trying to pressure us.

[   ]

Yes, sorry, you. They're trying to pressure you.

[   ]

No, no. No. It doesn't matter if they've given you an ultimatum—

[   ]

No. It just proves they're worried.

[   ]

Exactly. We make them wait.

[   ]

That's just a threat. They won't do anything. You just sit tight. Tell 'em you're thinking it over. That's all you have to do. Remember what I said about the tape?

[   ]

Exactly. I said don't use it. And was I right?

[   ]

It doesn't matter if it was real or not. That's not the point. The important thing was not to make an issue of it. You don't say anything. You don't have to say anything. You let it circulate and people will talk about it anyway. Something like that, it doesn't matter where it comes from.

[   ]

Yeah, but it worked, remember?

[   ]

Frank? Are you still there, Frank?

[   ]

No. You still sound terrible. Are you under a bridge? Don't tell them anything. Even if you think you can get a better deal—

[   ]

No. Don't ask for anything. Wait until they—

[   ]

Because they're scared. Why else would they offer you the job in the first place?

[ ]

No. You've got to be realistic here. It wasn't because of that.

[ ]

No, I'm not saying you couldn't win. It's just—

[ ]

Look, you can't win that ward. You've said it yourself.

[ ]

Yes you did.

[ ]

You did, Frank.

[ ]

No, I can't remember exactly when. But you've said it.

[ ]

No, I'm not saying that.

[ ]

Look, forget that. Forget that. The point is that they've offered you this for a reason.

[ ]

No, that's not the reason either.

[ ]

Look, I'm not. You might turn out to be the greatest director they've had since – since whenever. But that's not why they're offering you the job.

[ ]

No, I'm not saying that, Frank.

[ ]

No, I'm not questioning your ability. All I'm saying—

[ ]

OK, OK. You'll make a great director. One of the best. Now, can we get to the point? The point is they're scared of you. That's why they're putting pressure on you now. And while they're scared you've got the upper hand. You don't have to declare until a week before the election. You can't win it, but you can make them lose. So you do nothing and see what else they offer you.

[   ]

I don't know, Frank. I don't think they can make you director for life. Not officially. And it would just be a title. You want something a little more useful. Like a chance to appoint—

[   ]

No, something more than that. You've already got a car. You're in one now.

[   ]

You're not? I thought you were on a car phone.

[   ]

Right. From the cellar.

[   ]

Is that safe? Never mind. If they're listening, they're listening. You were saying you wanted what?

[   ]

I know they're good cars. I just don't think—

[   ]

You mean they haven't offered that already? I thought that was part of the deal.

[   ]

Grayford is a snake. As if you could accept without that.

[   ]

No, control of the budget would be definitely worth having. I don't deny that. But you don't ask for it.

[   ]

Because if you ask for something they'll know what to refuse. You have to let them offer it. And when you accept, do it like you're doing them a favour.

[   ]

If they give you a deadline, you just remind them they've still got a by-election. Remember, you can still fuck up their campaign.

[ ]

No, you can't win it.

[ ]

Because that's not why they're doing this. I've told you why, Frank.

[ ]

Grayford's nobody. Braddon's the one behind everything. We've got to be clever about this.

[ ]

No, I don't think you're being – I didn't say that, Frank. I said we had to be clever. That doesn't mean—

[ ]

Listen to me. What did I say about the tape? And was I right? Was I right?

[ ]

I was right, thank you. So you say nothing. You see what they offer. If you must say something ask about their reorganisation. Put them on their guard. Ask what their plans are for Parks.

[ ]

No, I don't. And I don't think they know themselves. I hear they've got all sorts of committees and sub-committees—

[ ]

You could, if you like that kind of thing. But you don't ask. You wait—

[ ]

No, we're in a strong position here. The worst they can do – politically – is to try and claim you went to them first. They'll probably—

[ ]

Look, I know you didn't. It's—

[   ]

No, Frank, I know you wouldn't, but—

[   ]

Not in a million, I know that. Look, it's me you're talking to, Frank. I'm just telling you the kind of trick they'll use. And it's nothing to worry about. I mean, who's going to believe them? We can win this. Do this right, you'll be laughing.

[   ]

Of course I do. I'm not doing this out of altruism.

Denise

Alan had moved into Jack's old office. As far as Denise could tell he hadn't made any changes. The room was as cluttered and impersonal as ever, a narrow room made narrower by the wooden filing cabinets that lined both sides. Jack's desk was approached as if along a corridor of paperwork. There were cardboard boxes of files stacked on the cabinets as well as on the floor beside and in front of them. The desk itself had come from a larger office and was nearly as wide as the room. Jack had always complained at having to squeeze round it – 'You'd think they'd have a smaller desk *somewhere*'. It was also covered with maps and pieces of paper. Behind the desk was a map of the administrative region on to which a street map of the town had been pinned. The street map, if nothing else, looked new.

Alan sat behind the desk. He wore glasses Denise had never seen before. They looked wrong on him, like an unsuccessful attempt at disguise. He was studying a piece of paper, his expression neutral, as if whatever was on the paper did not concern him and he was only reading it to while away the hours.

She said, 'Is this a good time?'

'There's no such thing as a good time.' He didn't look away from the paper. 'Close the door.'

She did as he said. 'I was last in this room two months ago.'

He looked up. His beard was more unkempt than usual and his dark hair was starting to curl at his temples. Was he allowing it to grow, or had he simply not been home? 'I know. I'd have preferred not to use this office, but ...' His tone suggested events beyond his control. He seemed to be asking her not to blame him. 'You can't always choose what you get. Sit down. Don't worry about the junk on the chair. Just put it on the floor.'

She did as he said. 'I see you've kept Jack's filing system.'

'I haven't had time to change anything.' He used a level, serious voice even with what should have been small talk. 'What with all the work on the toll roads. Now that's out of the way we're supposed to be preparing for the restructuring.'

'Don't they have to win the election first?'

'They're confident. It's usually a safe ward, and the toll roads are supposed to take care of any disaffection.'

'So the tape was right.'

'The tape was a fraud.' He frowned. 'How did you hear it? Was it through Jack?'

'Audit had a copy.'

The answer seemed to worry him, as if Audit's having a copy was a problem he hadn't foreseen. 'That tape could have caused us trouble. Did you bring the file?'

She passed over the cardboard folder. 'That's as much as I can let you see.'

'Have you read it yourself?'

'Of course I have.'

Again, she sensed his disapproval. He opened the folder. There were eight closely typed pages. 'There isn't much.'

'That's just the abstract. The whole file is over three hundred pages.'

He started to read. 'It would have been useful to see that.'

'You don't have the authorisation.'

He seemed about to dispute this, then to think better of it. 'As long as it's an accurate summary.' He turned to the second page. 'A lot of denunciations.'

'Not really.' Denise tried not to sound surprised. 'That's about an average number. The difference there is the quality. Most denunciations are rubbish – usually no more than vague allegations. There were some of those as well, but the ones I've included are specific. The sources are reliable.'

'You don't name them.'

'They're reliable.'

'I see. I suppose you're right to protect them, but it would have been useful.' He looked up. 'Am I the first person to have seen this?'

'No.'

It was another disappointment for him. 'I suppose you can't tell me who has seen it.'

'Audit Directorate, for a start.'

'I suppose they had to. Anybody else?'

'Come on, Alan. You know I can't tell you.'

He nodded, as if this confirmed his suspicion. 'It says it originated with a third party request. So who requested it, then? Army?'

'I can't tell you.'

'Amex? That might make sense. What with their land grab at the stadium.' He read on. 'Now, this is where it starts to get interesting. These people, do we know anything about them?'

She knew the names he was pointing at: Tunstall, Casteletti, Greaves. 'They're already under investigation.'

'The connection exists, then.'

'Between what?'

'If Tunstall and Greaves are Henderson associates,' he said, as if it should have been obvious, 'then that confirms what I expected.'

'I don't follow. Just because there's a connection with one of them—'

'It would be unlikely if there wasn't a connection, Denise. Somebody who knows Tunstall almost certainly knows Henderson.'

'That's a large assumption, Alan.'

'It's a necessary one, Denise.'

She let it go. Alan was stubborn: this was an argument she'd have to take elsewhere. 'So, what happens now?'

He smiled – like, she thought, a schoolboy who'd been waiting for just this question. 'What happens now is that I take this information to the right quarters. Then Transport will take action to dismantle the existing Parks leadership structure.' He glowed with pleasure. 'There's a rumour Henderson's going to be offered the directorship. It might be a good idea to clear out potential supporters. We can't let him have any real authority.'

'It's more than a rumour. As far as Audit's concerned the offer has been made and he's accepted.'

'Really?' He struggled to control his surprise. 'I would have expected to have been told if that were the case.'

'It's not yet official. It won't be announced until election day.'

'Should you have told me?' He looked anxious again. 'They must have been keeping it back for a reason.'

'Why shouldn't I? You'd have found out eventually.'

'That's not—' He stopped himself. 'I'm surprised he's taken it – if what you say is correct.' He struggled to see the positive side. 'He must have been getting some bad advice. He'll be right where they want him.'

She didn't want to talk about Henderson. 'Are you sure Transport can handle this?'

'We always handle problems with Parks.'

'This is a sensitive case, Alan.'

He almost smirked. 'I *have* thought about this, Denise. Doug will have personal responsibility for bringing in Kieran.'

'Doug? Won't that make it look personal?'

'Doug will handle it delicately. He can do that sort of thing.' Alan went on reading the abstract as he spoke, like a good bureaucrat. 'He's not as bad as people think. We have to shut this thing down quickly, before they know we know.'

'But you have to do it carefully.'

'We will be careful. But the council needs to demonstrate that it is in control. We can't allow this sort of department within a department to thrive. It's simply a matter of internal discipline.'

He spoke calmly, as if this was no more than an administrative reshuffle, a matter to be dealt with between an afternoon meeting and a coffee break. It was the kind of nonchalance that was reassuring when it was on your side.

He skimmed the rest of the file. 'I'd like to look at this in more detail later. How is Jack?'

'Better.' Denise was surprised by the question. 'He's talking again.'

'Really? What is he saying?'

'So far either yes or no. Don't worry, he's not asking for his job back.'

For a moment Alan looked offended; then he seemed to remember they were friends, and this was the kind of thing a friend might say. 'That's good, that he's talking.'

'It's a start. I can't let you keep the file.'

He put the papers down and sat back in his chair. 'You know, I'm sorry it's worked out like this.'

'Like what?'

He gestured at the maps on the wall and the filing cabinets. 'This. I won't deny I wanted Jack's job. But I didn't expect to get it like this. I thought he'd be promoted.'

'Well, that's not going to happen now.'

'But to get the job because of this.'

'Apologising to me doesn't help, Alan.'

'You're right, but you do understand how I feel, don't you?'

Denise was no longer surprised when people told her how terrible they felt about Jack. They meant well, or wanted to seem to mean well, but gave the impression they believed *their* feelings were what mattered, as if she was supposed to comfort *them*. 'Right now, Alan, I'm more concerned with how this will affect Siobhan.'

Alan looked down at the file. 'I believe she's involved.'

'With what?'

'Kieran's activities.'

'I doubt that.'

'I don't.' Alan reverted to his official voice. 'At the very least she must have known. It's not as if she was some downtrodden Scoomer wife whose husband doesn't talk to her.'

'There's no mention of her involvement in the file.'

'There doesn't have to be. I'd say it was fairly certain. Do you know she visited Jack in the hospital?'

'So? She's a friend.'

'We posted an extra guard. He saw it. I wonder why she went. Does Audit keep a record?'

'Not of that ward. Look, she probably went because Jack's a friend.'

'That's one interpretation. I think she went to report back to Kieran. She's just as guilty.'

'Hang on, Alan. If she wanted to find out about Jack she could have asked us. And if Kieran wanted to know he could have found out for himself.'

He frowned, as if these were trivial objections. 'We can argue about this, Denise, but I'd rather be safe than sorry.'

'Safe? Are you saying Siobhan is a threat?'

'This isn't about her being a threat.' His voice was level, but it cost him an effort, as if, faced with her unreasonable questions, he found it difficult to remain calm. 'It's about containing a problem.'

'Is it?' But this was a decision he'd already made. Denise could see there was no room for argument. 'So what are you planning to do?'

'First, we need to remove Kieran from post. Also' – tapping the file – 'we need to keep an eye on these people. We need to do it with a minimum of fuss. Now, as Siobhan knows about Kieran's activities it's pretty certain she knows about his associates, including the ones that haven't made it into our files. I don't want to have her warning them. These people could be in positions of authority with access to firearms. We can't take the risk of a public disturbance.'

'Are you sure you're not overreacting?'

'This is a serious matter, Denise. This kind of activity' – again, he tapped the folder – 'could undermine the authority of the council. And I don't want to see a return to the situation we had ten years ago.'

'Siobhan is one of our friends. She may have had nothing to do with this.'

'Denise, I have to work on the assumption that she does. It would be irresponsible of me not to.'

'A friend, Alan.'

'I appreciate what you're saying, Denise, and it isn't easy for me.' But he didn't make it sound difficult either: he sounded as if this was the kind of work that made his job worthwhile. 'Remember, we thought Kieran was a friend as well. And I can't allow a presumption of one person's innocence to lead to what could be a serious disturbance.' He softened his tone, as if as a concession to her weakness. 'I'll tell them to be careful.'

'And remember you're dealing with an Amex employee. They can be very protective. You don't want a truckload of their security turning up at your office.'

'It will be done professionally. We'll pick her up at home.'

'Let Doug handle it.'

'Oh, we shouldn't need him. Siobhan is only dangerous because of her associations, she's hardly dangerous herself.

We can use regular staff.'

'Are you enjoying this, Alan?'

He looked hurt. It was the same expression he had when he talked about his family. When he spoke his words had the same rote quality: 'I don't know how you can even think that. I didn't ask for this responsibility, but it has fallen to me, as you know, and I am going to serve the public interest to the best of my ability. If that means I have to do some things that I find personally difficult, well, they have to be done. And I'm not going to apologise for doing what I think is the right thing.'

Denise stood up. She had seen Alan like this before. He had convinced himself he was right and would take any disagreement as an attack on his cherished integrity. There was no arguing with him when that happened. All she could do now was file a report to Audit Directorate, expressing reservations about T & E's approach. 'I'd better get back to my office. I'll need the file. I should warn you, Kieran does have contacts. He knew someone had asked to see his records.'

Alan reluctantly closed the folder and handed it back to her. 'This doesn't mention any contact in Audit.'

'There's a lot that goes undocumented.'

'Audit needs reorganisation. They'll be next, you know.'

'No.' She started walking towards the door. 'We just need to be properly staffed.'

'I think a change in working practices ...'

She closed the door on him before he could finish.

Our readers will be aware that to get anything done in this town it is necessary to know a councillor, and that such knowledge comes at a price. Your columnist has recently heard a story illustrative of this very process. Now, our council has plans for this town: committees and sub-committees have been formed to Investigate Issues and Make Recommendations. Naturally our councillors seek to influence their deliberations. One councillor – our readers will guess which one – wanted a certain person removed from one of these committees; this councillor spoke to Someone in Parks, whereupon an unofficial roadblock manned by Parks and Libraries staff ensured that the unfortunate committee member is now recovering in hospital, his place at the table taken – surprise! – by none other than a nephew of the councillor. Audit are asked to conduct one of their usually feared investigations; on this occasion, however, it turns out that the Someone in Parks has a close personal friendship with the auditor chosen to lead the investigation. Your columnist is not optimistic that the guilty party will ever be named. The responsibility will doubtless be deflected on to those poor souls who thought they were following orders, but will soon find they were acting on their own initiative.

Does this sound unduly cynical? Dear readers, this is how business is done in our town. A bargain is struck in a back room, a few lives are ruined, and the council then finds it is innocent of all wrongdoing. Nobody should be surprised.

Meanwhile, the campaign for Councillor Goss's old ward has begun in earnest. A sign of this heightened activity is that this week's issue is once again later than advertised. The cause this time is not the usual one of interrupted supplies, but a fire in the corrugated iron shed we liked to think of as our office – a fire, we believe, that was not started by accident. Was this fire the result of innocent vandalism or something more sinister? We do not like to speculate. After all, with an election so close, we should expect the occasional barricade and house fire. And *The Report* has ruffled enough feathers in this town merely by asking awkward questions.

Needless to say, it will take more than a single fire to silence this publication, just as it will take more than a toothless report on the death of Councillor Goss to convince us there isn't more to the story. Your columnist is not concerned with rumours about reckless driving or careless gunplay. How the councillor met his fiery end is less important than the question of what he was doing on the road that night. Where was he going? Where had he been? There has been vague talk about 'council business', but official sources have given scant corroborating details. Indeed, the idea of our councillors engaging in official business at that time of night is laughable, when, as our readers are aware, they do so little in office hours.

But all that, as officialdom will tell you, is ancient history. We have all heard the excuses: what's done is done, we must deal with present problems, there is no point dwelling on the past, we must look to the future, etc. – anything to keep us from finding out what actually happened. Mea culpa, readers: your columnist has repeated stories as readily as any gossip in a drinking house, but we cannot live on rumours and suppositions. He does not suggest that we embrace the millennial certainties of Councillor Harding's followers, but he would like to know, for once, what is actually happening in this town. Last week, on the day we should have gone to press, there was another gas explosion in the fetid warren by the seafront. It was the fourth this year. That is our town in an election week: gas explosions and random fires, and nobody can quite say why anything is happening. But the election does bring some hope – not in the outcome itself, which will be the usual consequence of a choice between evils, but in the presence of the observers. There is always the faint chance that one of them may raise his or her head above the fence of their compound, or hear the voice of somebody who is not a council interpreter, and, astonishingly, actually observe.

Bystander

Margaret

Margaret had never liked elections. They were too disruptive. Barricades – not always official – could appear without warning, and no matter how many people were rounded up on the morning there were always *incidents*. The whole town would smell of things burning and the next day there would be rubble and broken glass everywhere – even, somehow, in those streets where nothing had been broken. Timetables became meaningless. Council workers – including people who should have known better – would spend the day spreading rumours while neglecting their own work. It would take weeks to clear the streets and patch up the damaged buildings. And then, after all the shouting and disruption, there would be days of celebration that would be nearly as bad.

Already, on her way to work that morning, she had seen two bodies. One, a thin man with a bloody head, had been propped against a shop doorway, like a beggar; a few yards further away, as if for contrast, a fat man lay face down in the gutter, his arms spread as if he was trying to swim there. A gang of youths had gathered outside the old cinema and had thrown bricks at the passing cars, narrowly missing her own. Her driver had laughed and called back, 'Are you blind?' Margaret had not been amused: T & E should have cleared that street; those children should have been held at the Goldstone pen until the election was over. Yet she hadn't seen a council uniform anywhere, apart from her driver's – and he was wrong to treat that kind of anarchy as a lark. Even at the council offices order seemed to have broken down: uniformed men sat on the floor of the lobby or leaned against walls, apparently waiting for orders. The phone lines, she discovered, had been cut. While queuing at the vending machine for coffee she heard that Amex security men had shut down the road to London, that Councillor Braddon had been shot by his secretary and that a bomb had been found in the Pavilion offices. She didn't believe any of these stories; she had heard them at other elections and it irritated her that her colleagues still found them worth repeating. Then, passing the office Louise occasionally shared with eight other people, she had noticed Louise standing by one of the desks, hugging another woman, one of the juniors, who seemed to be in tears. Margaret thought this was overreacting: anybody would have thought they were saying goodbye for ever. Louise was wrong to encourage this kind of sloppy emotionalism. Margaret would have spoken to her if she hadn't already been so late. The corridors were filled with frightened, excited people. The lifts were out of order – but that was normal, you couldn't blame the election for that. On the staircase on Level B she saw two senior officers actually fighting, one man swinging his arms wildly while the other clung to his lapels and screamed into his face. If she could have remembered their names she would have reported them. Finally, a little short of breath from the stairs, she reached Level F, Room 24. The guard straightened from his slouch as soon as he saw Margaret and opened the door.

Kieran didn't look up when Margaret entered the room. She had to say his name aloud before he noticed she was there. He showed no surprise. 'You.' Then, with a smile: 'Why are you here? I haven't got any kids for you to take away.'

Margaret sat at the other side of the table. 'That's not what I do.'

'Oh?' Kieran smiled as if it was natural for them to meet like this. She noticed his lip was split and wondered if he'd resisted. 'And what is it you do, Lou?'

'I talk to people.' She would not let herself be charmed by him. 'I make assessments.'

'I thought Audit did that kind of thing. I thought they had the specialists.'

'Did you.' He was still in uniform. They'd probably let him finish his shift before bringing him in. There were other marks on his face that would soon look worse. 'That isn't how it works. We're not Parks. Transport brings you in, Welfare processes.'

'Processes. You make it sound so formal, Mags.'

'This is formal.' Bravado. He was trying to make this personal, as if there was a bottle of wine on the table between them, and Alan beside her. Well it wouldn't work. Margaret wasn't about to ask how he was, or complain about the chaos outside. She understood there was a difference between her private life and her public duty. 'Do you know why you're here?'

The same easy smile. 'Politics.'

'You're in breach of regulations.'

'That's just an excuse, Mags, and you know it. This is all about the reorganisation. Grayford wants to take over Parks so he's getting rid of people he thinks will cause trouble.'

'That's not the issue here.'

'And what is the issue, Mags?'

'Stability. We don't want this town to go back to what it was.'

'Ten years ago. I've heard that.' He smiled crookedly. Someone had punched his mouth, probably because he'd smiled with too much assurance. He didn't seem to have lost any teeth. 'It's always ten years ago. Ten years ago it was terrible, and now it's – well, what do you think this town is turning into, Mags? A little beacon of democracy and civic order?'

'This isn't about my opinion.'

'It's a racket, Mags. It's all just a racket.'

It was usually difficult to make people talk. Either Kieran didn't understand his situation, or he understood and didn't care. She said: 'Kieran, I am not here as your friend.'

'I didn't for one minute imagine you were.'

'Do you know why I'm talking to you?'

His smile vanished. 'Mags, do you think I care?'

'My job is to determine whether an individual is a suitable case for council support. We have only finite resources. In a case like yours we have to decide whether we deal with it internally or pass it on to the external authorities.'

He yawned ostentatiously. 'You don't have to tell me, Mags. If you want to hand me over to whoever, just do it. You don't have to recite your job description.'

She stared at him. How could he be so wrong? 'At the moment we're more inclined to treat this as a matter for internal discipline.'

'Unpaid leave.' He grinned again. 'I can live with that.'

'That's not what happens.'

'What?' His eyes widened with mock horror. 'You don't think they'll give me the sack, do you?'

'No.' When people were flippant, the best approach was to pretend to take them seriously. 'Your contract doesn't allow for that. Your case is likely to be treated in-house.'

This had its effect. Kieran's expression went blank, as if he wasn't sure how to respond. He decided on glum defiance. 'And what is my case, Mags? What am I supposed to have done?'

'You know.'

'I don't know, Mags. What regulations am I supposed to have breached? Other than the ones everybody breaches.'

'You want me to list them? You authorised the use of council resources to assist illegal smuggling operations.'

He snorted. 'That's desperate. Has Al paid the full duty on his little wine cellar?'

She ignored him. 'You have political associations that could lead to a clear conflict of interest.'

'And who doesn't?'

'You exceeded your authority by ordering a Parks operation in a Transport area. You attempted to influence the outcome of an internal investigation. That's what we know already. I suspect we'll find more if we go deeper.'

'No. This is about politics, Mags. I know it and you know it.' He was subdued, as if he was withdrawing into himself, preparing himself for his next move. She was glad there was a table between them, and a guard at the door. 'All I did is what everybody else does. This is all about Grayford getting rid of people he thinks will cause trouble. It's about the restructuring.'

'You're in breach of regulations.'

His smile again. He'd thought of something. 'Alan must love this.'

'This has nothing to do with him.'

'Is that what you think? I know why I'm really here, Mags. You think I had something to do with what happened to poor old Jack.'

'A serious assault.'

'I heard nothing was broken.' Kieran touched his own damaged lip. 'No, Mags. I had nothing to do with that.'

'We have proof.'

'No you don't. There isn't any. It all comes back to Grayford. The question you've got to ask is: who benefited? *Cui bono*, eh?'

'It was your attempt to influence an internal—'

He slammed his open palm down on the table, smiling when she flinched. 'If I'd wanted to intimidate Denise I wouldn't have wasted time on Jack. They can't stand each other anyway. Grayford wanted Jack off the committee. Jack was too independent for him. So who's going to replace him?'

The guard looked into the room. Margaret waved him away. 'The officer you approached has stated that—'

'Ma'am.' The guard was still at the door. He nodded at the corridor.

'It can wait.' Margaret tried to hide her irritation. 'I will be finished in a few minutes.' She turned back to Kieran, who raised his eyebrows.

'I'm sorry, ma'am,' the guard persisted. 'They say it's important.'

'You'd better go,' Kieran said. 'If it's important. Don't worry about me. I'll still be here.'

'I won't be long.'

'Of course not, Mags. You're efficient.'

She left him, and found the serious matter was no more than a messenger with paperwork that needed her signature – hers, because nobody else was available. Even Louise, who could have signed them, had apparently left the office.

Tutting, Margaret glanced through the reports. Five people, found in the ward where the election was being held, suspected of trying to *disrupt the democratic process*. She didn't recognise any of the names, but then she only remembered the difficult cases. Four of the detainees claimed to have no political affiliations, the fifth was a Helmstoner: a surprise, because it was rare for them to travel alone. She was unlikely to have been a threat, Margaret decided, and might simply have been lost. She could be released once the polls closed. The others could be held for further questioning.

They were simple decisions that could have been delegated to juniors, but Margaret still felt a little jolt of pleasure at her own competence. She handed the files back to the messenger and returned to the room.

Kieran sat in the same position she had left him. 'See, Mags? I said you were efficient. So what was it that was so important?'

'It's not your concern.'

'How can you be sure?'

'It has been reported that you made threats.'

He sighed heavily and leaned back in his chair. 'Were you assigned this job, Mags, or did you request it?'

'That's not the issue here.'

'It is for me. You see, of course I spoke to Denise. I'd heard someone was interested in my file and I wanted to find out why. Who wouldn't? So I asked a friend, just like anybody else would. Jack had nothing to do with me.'

'The men were under your command.'

'Them and a hundred others. They were off duty. Moonlighting. I can't control what people do in their spare time.' He said it as if he meant it. Margaret could see how other people might find that convincing. That was why it was necessary for them not to see him. 'Besides, as I said, you have to look at who benefited from it. Who got the promotion? And what are his connections?'

'That's not the issue.'

'It's exactly the issue. Because you're connected, Mags. This one leads to your house. Yours, Mags. And if Parks gets disbanded and T and E takes over, who gets even more power? That's the question you should be asking. You say I'm in breach of the regulations, but honestly, Mags, so fucking what? You have to break the rules just to live in this town. But that's not the real story, is it? You talk about the rules, but the real story is that this is personal.'

'Nonsense.'

'Alan gives the order and you *process* me and I'm supposed to think it's an accident? Do you know who he sent to pick me up? Doug. Doug, Mags. How is that not personal?'

She stood up. 'Guard.' She knew the guard's name: Ben Hooley. She'd recruited him five years earlier. His parents had been alcoholics. By some chance, he hadn't been. She'd felt sorry for him, a confused twelve-year-old, big for his age, barely able to read or write his own name. She'd had him assigned to a place on a training programme. He was one of her success stories.

Ben stood by the door, his reddish face somehow both blank and eager. 'Ma'am?'

'The interview is over.'

Kieran laughed bitterly. 'Do I get the job?'

Margaret didn't look at him. 'I've learned what I need to know.'

'I'm sure you have. And I'm sure they can trust you to reach the right decision.'

'Yes,' she said. 'They can.'

For a moment, his show of confidence faltered. 'And what have you decided?'

She stepped away from the table. 'That this is best treated as an in-house matter.'

'And what does that mean?'

Ben stood aside to let her pass. She stopped at the door and turned back. 'That will be decided at cabinet.'

'By Grayford, I suppose.'

'He does have a vote.'

'Do you think your opinion counts in this, Mags? Grayford's already decided.'

She left him in his cell. It had been an easy decision made, like all her decisions, within the first few seconds. She had never, she told herself, liked Kieran. He had been an outsider, and she had known from the beginning he would never fit in. It was gratifying to have official confirmation. Now all that remained was to write the report.

She realised he had not mentioned Siobhan once.

Transcript #32117

So what happened, John. What the fuck happened?

We have the results. I think—

Didn't go according to your master plan, did it, Grayford?

There was nothing wrong with my [   ]

Except it didn't work.

[   ]

What was that, old man?

I don't appreciate your tone, Mr Plaice.

I don't want your appreciation. This is your fucking fault.

I think it's a little early to start apportioning blame, Geoff.

Well I don't. We lost, John. Do you know what – well, you know as well as I do what. It means we've lost the majority.

It's not as bad as that.

Shut it, Grayford.

You'd be in a worse position without me.

How could we be, you useless old fart? How could we be worse, we lost for fuck's sake. We followed your advice and turned a solid lead into a fuck. Fuck.

Calm down, Geoff.

Calm down? Calm? I think this is – that there are things that need to be said. Fuck. Fuck.

Please, Geoff.

OK, John. OK. So what happened to our ward?

As I've been trying to explain, it's still too early to tell, but the first reports indicate—

Don't look at me like that, Grayford.

Please, Geoff.

Look at him. He's sitting there, looking at me.

You're nothing, Plaice. You're a cheap little [   ]

Cheap! You can talk, with your [   ]

[   ]

Gentlemen, please, can we save the arguments for later? The first reports, as I was saying, the first reports indicate that Labour seem to have benefited from an exceptionally low turnout.

So where were our voters? Bastards.

The first indications are, you, you will recall, there was heavy traffic that day.

So you're saying they were stuck in traffic?

It's too early to say with certainty—

[   ]

Not at all, Miles. The adjustments to the toll roads were in place, exactly—

[   ]

Please, gentlemen. In fact— What. This is a private meeting – oh, Miss Harding, we weren't expecting you. Sunday and all.

I have fulfilled my obligations to the Lord.

Good for him. John was telling us why Grayford's plan didn't work.

I have heard the result, Mr Plaice.

As have we all, Miss Harding. Now, as I was saying—

Thanks to Grayford's plan our voters were stuck in traffic.

That's possibly a simplification, Geoff, but it is possible that the toll road adjustments were part of the problem.

See? I fucking knew it.

Please, Geoff, let me finish. The adjustments were made known two weeks ago, with the usual minimum publicity. The idea, you'll remember, was that drivers should find out for themselves that it was possible to – well, they did. And that seems to have been part of the problem.

There can't be that many fucking cars in the [   ]

There aren't, Geoff. Not to cause the kind of delays we saw. The problem seems to have arisen when motorists from other wards discovered there was now an essentially toll-free corridor, and started going out of their way to use it. The pressure started building on the system—

So we can say it is T and E's fault.

As well as yours, Grayford.

So we sack the people responsible.

I'll come to that, Miles. The roads, that particular stretch, had been getting busier—

Shouldn't T and E have noticed this? Isn't that what they're supposed to do?

Well, yes, Geoff, they did have systems in place to monitor the flow of traffic, but it seems that on this occasion, unfortunately—

They weren't doing their job. You know, for once I agree with Grayford. Sack the bastards.

[   ] who was responsible for this?

[   ]

Mr Plaice, if—

I'm sorry, Miss Harding – but you haven't read the report, have you, Grayford?

[   ]

Miles?

[   ]

Grayford, you've changed colour.

In light of this, I think – I think perhaps sacking would be premature.

Hang on, Miles, you said – oh, I get it. I see.

Miles, Councillor, I don't understand.

Grayford's recognised a name, Miss Harding. The man responsible for not noticing the, the – the man whose only job was to count the fucking cars, that man. Familiar is it, Grayford?

As Councillor Braddon has said—

Who, who, who could that man be?

Too early to blame individuals—

Not your day, is it, Grayford?

If this is true, Miles—

Look, Miss Harding, John, it's clear to me that there's no point allowing ourselves to get bogged down in this kind of, kind of administrative detail. The issue here isn't about finding a scapegoat but how we solve this—

But I like this detail, Grayford. I think we should dwell on it. At length.

[   ], Plaice.

Oh look, he's angry. Mind your blood pressure, Grayford.

There is nothing wrong with [   ]

Please, Miles, Geoff. If we can return to the matter at hand. The roads were getting busier and busier, very busy in fact, until on the day of the election—

Gridlocked. See, Grayford? That's where your plan—

[   ]

Please, Geoff. Don't hit the table. The real problems started when a lorry broke down just outside Moulsecoomb, which closed one lane, and then shortly afterwards two cars were involved in a collision—

Fucking Christ.

Mr Plaice, I must object to your language.

Oh fuck off, you old bat.

Mr Plaice, there is really no need—

There's every need. Fuck, we've just lost a by-election in what should have been a safe ward and you're worried about my language? Fucking Christ.

It's not over yet.

Still breathing, Grayford?

Do Labour know the results yet?

Here comes another master plan.

If you can't be constructive, Mr Plaice—

Thank you, Miss Harding. I am just trying to get us out of this—

This mess that you've got us into. No thanks.

Gentlemen, please. Miles, what you're thinking won't work. Labour already know the results.

And we know they're fair? We can't question the count?

Miles, you're clutching at – well, they're not even straws. Contesting the – it isn't going to help us.

But the observers! If we could get them—

They won't care, Miles. We [   ]

[   ] giving up too easily. But I think it's clear the fault with this actually lies—

That's right, Grayford. With anyone but you.

There was nothing wrong with my plan.

Well obviously, because it worked so well.

You endorsed it, Plaice.

Reluctantly. You're more to blame than T and E, Grayford.

I couldn't have known—

[   ]

[   ]

Please, both of you. To be fair to T and E, this wasn't their fault. They did exactly what we told them. And while they could have made a better job of monitoring the traffic—

So you're blaming me as well, John, is that it?

Please, Miles, I'm not here to apportion blame.

I am.

Geoff, this isn't perhaps the time. Now, as I was saying, there were unprecedented traffic jams that day. It's speculated that many of our voters may have arrived at their bases late, which meant they were obliged to work late to make up the hours. There was then even worse congestion on the evening run, and, as you know, the majority of votes are cast in the evening.

So? We must have realised something was going wrong. Couldn't we have kept the polls open?

Closing them at nine was something you supported, Geoff.

[   ] doesn't mean I support them in a case like [   ]

Mind your blood pressure, Plaice.

Shut it, Grayford.

Don't hit the table, Geoff, it interferes with the—

I'll [   ] the [   ] table if I like. Surely, surely, we must have had someone there who noticed something was [   ]

Geoff, we couldn't have done anything on the night, without provoking real trouble.

So? What are T and E for?

We don't want a return to the situation of ten years ago.

No. Instead we've lost our majority. We've got a hung council. Which means, Grayford, we won't be able to push through your restructuring. And do you know what else?

Calm down, Geoff.

I will not calm down, John. I think some anger is appropriate. We won't be able to push through your restructuring, Grayford, and do you know what that means?

[   ]

Haven't guessed yet? Henderson.

[   ] not a problem.

He's in charge of Parks. And now Parks isn't going to be merged. And we've got Amex on our backs over some typist.

I believe she was more than a typist—

I'm sure she was, John. Because somebody's favourite nephew got a bit trigger-happy—

That's an outrageous [   ]

[   ] witnesses, Grayford. It happened on their patch. They want blood.

Nathan told me. He explained.

He had one thing to do. One thing.

A simple mistake—

Go to somebody's house, with a guard, and pick up one person – one person, John – before they left for work. What could be simpler?

There were difficult [   ]

[   ] possibly get it wrong? The answer is, the same way he fucked up everything else.

[   ] situation. The election [   ]

[   ] his job to know the roads would be blocked! So he goes to her house, but he's too late. So he thinks she's left for work. So he drives to their compound, sees her about to go through the gates, and what [   ]

It wasn't his [   ]

[   ] panics! Shoots her! In full view of their security! In full view! Do you know what that is going to cost us?

Look, we don't know that this woman wasn't a serious threat.

Yes we do, Grayford. We know she wasn't a serious threat. Because she wasn't the [   ]

[   ]

[   ] the wrong woman! The one he's supposed to pick up – gone! Left on an Amex security convoy earlier that day. She's probably not even in the country. But this idiot, he reaches the gates, sees a woman, assumes it's her, and shoots. In full view of their security. It's a complete [   ]

Look, if this other woman is now out of the country then she's no longer a problem.

That's not the point, Grayford!

And if you're worried about Amex, that isn't a problem. We've dealt with this kind of thing before. They want the old stadium, we let them have it. We don't need it. We barely filled the Goldstone this time round. They'll soon forget this woman. It's business.

You don't get it, do you, Grayford? The stadium belongs to Parks. It's Henderson's now, remember? It's not ours to give away!

He'll do what we tell him.

Shut up, Grayford. Just shut up. You've lost us the election, given a major department to a man who hates us, and pissed off the biggest [ ] in the county.

Amex can be dealt with and Henderson isn't a problem.

You still don't get it, do you?

[ ] won't be a problem, Plaice. He won't control the budget.

Actually, Miles, you may remember—

[ ]

I still don't see—

[ ] just removed a whole team of senior officers because they supported him! Now you've put the man himself in charge!

Geoff, please.

Don't please me, John. Grayford's plan has been a fucking disaster.

Mr Plaice, I do think—

Fuck! Fuck! Fuck! Fuck!

[ ]

Geoff, there's no need – are you all right?

Switch it off!

[ ]

Oh dear. He looks—

    . [ ] off!

Geoff? Geoff?

How's your blood pressure now, Plaice?

Miles, I don't think this is the time. Geoff, are you all right?

    [ ]

It is a judgement, Mr Plaice.

Miss Harding, this is not the time. He needs help.

    [ ]

O Lord, look down from heaven—

Miss Harding, what are you doing?

    [ ] the only true help.

Well do something useful instead. Get the guard! Geoff! Can you hear me?

    [ ]

Miles, at least help me. If we can get him to his feet—

    [ ]

Break not the bruised reed.

Miss Harding! Geoff? On the table. Can you hear me, Geoff?

    [ ]

    [ ] the smoking flax.

Just go, Miss Harding! Get the guard!

    [ ]

Honestly, that woman is [ ]. Geoff? Geoff? Hang on, Geoff. We're getting help. I don't know what you're smiling about, Miles. The last thing we need is another by——

    [ ]

    [ ]

    [ ]

So the by-election is finally over. The observers have left for the capital, the 'known troublemakers' have been released from the holding pens, and, as is the tradition here, a number of our citizens now find themselves, through little fault of their own, out of work. Our favourite councillor's favourite nephew is, we hear, among these unfortunates. We do not know the reason for it, and none, of course, will be given, though we have heard rumours of what the authorities like to call *an incident*.

His latest spell of unemployment, however, is expected to last no longer than any of his others. It is said the scamp may soon be donning the drab green of the recently reorganised Parks and Libraries. He is said to be reluctant, but where else can he go? No other department offers work commensurate with his talents, and his family connections count for nothing with our town's other employer. Even if it is true that they are looking to fill the gap left by the sudden departure of some of their brighter staff they are unlikely to want this particular young man – except, possibly, as a hostage. And so he will go to Parks. Who knows? Perhaps that department's eccentric new chief will find in him a kindred spirit. Perhaps he will turn into a worthwhile public servant after all. We at *The Report* are nothing if not optimistic.

Next week's edition, dear readers, will be delayed for the usual reasons.

Bystander

Acknowledgements

I owe an obvious debt to Candida Lacey and Vicky Blunden and the rest of the team at Myriad. Without their efforts and enthusiasm this book would simply not exist in its present form. Apart from that, thanks are due to (among others) Naomi Foyle, Louise Halvardsson, David Hellens, Rob Johnston, Karen Miles, and Kay Sexton for their support and encouragement.

AFTERWORD:

ABOUT ROBERT DICKINSON :

Were you encouraged to read widely as a child?
We weren't discouraged. If nothing else, it kept us quiet.

What was your favourite subject at school?
Art. I liked painting and drawing, without being particularly good at either.

Did you write compulsively as a child?
Not until my teens. But I was a compulsive reader – hyperlexic, even.

What is the first book you remember reading?
I remember being struck by hearing *The Pilgrim's Progress* read aloud at Sunday school. For books that I read for myself, there were children's abridged editions of classics like *Treasure Island*, *The Last of the Mohicans*, and *Jane Eyre*, which I found baffling but somehow alluring.

What do you do when you are not writing?
Reading, watching television, shopping, listening to music. Thinking, 'I should be writing.'

Which authors do you most admire?
It would be a long list. Let's say Penelope Fitzgerald, William Gaddis, Mary McCarthy and Wallace Stevens, for starters.

What would you be if you weren't a writer?
Wealthier.

Which book do you wish you had written?
I'm tempted to say *The Da Vinci Code*. Then I could retire and finish *The Book of Disquiet*.

Do you have a favourite book?
It changes from month to month. Recent favourites have been Helen DeWitt's *The Last Samurai* and Amy Clampitt's *Collected Poems*.

What do you look for in a novel?
It depends on the novel. You can't read Curtis White in the same way you'd read Anne Tyler. I suppose I prefer a certain coolness of tone.

What is your greatest extravagance?
Buying books in languages that I can't yet read, and CDs I don't listen to until months or years later.

What is the trait you most deplore in yourself?
Idleness.

What words or phrases do you most overuse?
'Do you have the purchase order number?'

What is your favourite word?
I've always liked 'permafrost'.

What is your least favourite word?
Lots of business and corporate-speak. I always think less well of people who say 'substantive'.

What is your guiltiest pleasure?
Anything that isn't writing.

Where else can readers find your work?
There's a collection of poems from Waterloo Press called *Micrographia*. And there's a CD from Signum Records of Tenebrae performing Joby Talbot's choral piece *Path of Miracles*, for which I assembled the text. I particularly like the music for the third movement, 'Leon'.

ABOUT THE NOISE OF STRANGERS :

How did you start the book?
I'd had an idea for the general atmosphere of the book for a long time.
It was only when I realised what the shape of the book would be that
I started writing.

How long did it take to write?
The first draft probably took about six months. The various revisions
probably took another year and a half. I was working on other things
as well.

What encouraged you along the way?
I had a sense that this was different from anything I'd done before.
All novels are set in some kind of alternative reality: this was the most
explicitly alternative, rather than pretending to be realistic.

How important was research to the writing of the book?
I was able to draw on a lot of things I already knew. I'd worked for
large organisations – both public and private – for years. I'd also had a
longstanding interest in a certain kind of politics, particularly in the old
Eastern Europe. In a sense, the book is the product of research that I
hadn't realised was research.

How did you find your characters?
They arose from the milieu. Their individual characteristics became
clearer as the book progressed.

Does the book have a moral message?
All stories enact the morality of the teller, so I suppose there's one in there
somewhere. There may even be several.

**In what ways did you draw on your own experiences while writing
the novel?**
The novel is in some ways the inevitable result of those experiences. The
various jobs I've had, and reflections on the nature of those jobs, play a
part, but usually indirectly.

Are any of the characters based on people you have known?
No. But with the usual caveat that they may contain elements of actual people.

How much do other sources influence your work?
A lot, and probably in ways I wouldn't notice. I am more likely to be influenced by books than films. I can't think of specific influences in this case, though it might be significant that I re-read both *1984* and *The Group* about the time I started writing. I'm also interested in the idea of a musical structure, in this case a series of variations on a ground – a series of episodes with a larger story ever present in the background. Of course, musical analogies break down very quickly. The nature of the medium – words – means you can't have a true counterpoint, or development, but only something loosely analogous.

How did you decide on the structure of the novel?
From the beginning I knew the novel would consist of a series of conversations between the members of four couples. Before I wrote a word of the first chapter I drew up a list of characters and the order of the chapters in which they would appear. In between each chapter there would be a document of some kind that would fill in the background and give these conversations their context.

What was most challenging about the writing of the novel?
Balancing the different elements. I didn't want the same characters to appear in successive chapters, or to have similar documents too close to each other. I also wanted to give an idea of their world without spelling out too much about it, which meant keeping exposition to a minimum. These characters live in this world: how often would they talk or think about it in a way helpful to outsiders? On the other hand, I didn't want to leave the reader completely baffled.

Why did you set the book in Brighton?
Because I wanted the novel to have a provincial quality: the action would not take place in the capital, the fate of the nation would not be at stake. Many of the characters feel trapped. And Brighton – particularly in this version of it – is small enough to feel claustrophobic and large enough to contain different social groups. And it helped that I lived there.

Did you feel it was important that the setting was recognisable?
The usual view of the town is that it's a lively, arty place – simultaneously stylish and ramshackle, swarming with visitors and flush with London money. Not much of that survives in this version, which, in itself, was a quick way of suggesting we are in a different world.

Was it a conscious decision to avoid physical description of your characters?
Yes. Not that I have anything against physical descriptions – one or two even managed to creep in before they were spotted and removed. But I find that when I read other novels I usually don't remember anything beyond general indications of appearance. The reader's impression of a character can quickly take over from the author's painstakingly elaborate descriptions.

Did you want to minimise the sense of an authorial voice in the book?
Again, yes. In very early drafts some scenes were presented completely externally, with no access to any of the characters' thoughts. I quickly realised this would be too alienating, and that there had to be more contrast with the various documents and transcripts that make up the rest of the novel.

Did you know how the book would end when you began it?
Mostly. Writing a novel has been compared to driving at night: you know where you want to go, but at any moment you can only see a little of the road ahead.

How did you decide on the ending?
I knew the main outline from quite early on. I wavered about the fate of some individuals.

Do you know what happens next for your characters?
Mostly.

How necessary is it that some characters who play an important role in the story don't actually appear in the book?
I wanted to give a sense of a society beyond that of the main characters. And there are different levels of not appearing: from being mentioned in reports to writing anonymous letters or being the unrecorded half of

a telephone conversation. But I like the idea of characters we only hear about at one remove having importance for their effects on other people. They're like those friends of friends we somehow never meet.

How did you decide on the kinds of technology that would feature in the book - and the kinds that wouldn't?
I wanted it to be, by our standards, low-tech. Mobile phones do not exist, the electricity is unreliable. When things break down they are patched up rather than replaced. The details are meant to suggest something about the state of the wider world.

Why did you choose to focus on the women from each couple in the narrative chapters?
I'd previously worked on a piece entirely from the perspective of male characters, in which women barely featured at all. Partly I wanted a contrast. And partly, as I started planning this novel, I felt that chapters written from the perspective of the men might have merged too seamlessly with some of the surrounding documents, which are mostly by, to, or about men. Not that I wanted to set up a neat women equals domesticity, men equals bureaucracy dichotomy (the women are as implicated in the system as the men).

How would you describe the temporal setting of the book?
Vaguely. It's obviously set in a world that has developed differently from our own. I do have a long and intricate back-story, but left it out because I didn't want to write an exercise in alternative history. I was more concerned with how the characters adapt to their situation.

Did you want the novel to raise questions about contemporary society and the complexities of local government in particular?
There are elements in the story that are plainly extrapolations from recent history. And the way the characters justify their actions, and their disdain for other social groups – these things are constants. That the authority takes the form it does has less to do with current trends. The central power here has the trappings of local government, but they are only the trappings. The nature of the institutions have changed but their names have remained the same. The authorities here are really closer to warlords, years after a negotiated truce. They're pretending to be democrats because that gives an illusion of legitimacy, which is where the money is.

Where does blame lie in the novel?
Almost all of the people who behave badly would behave better if their circumstances were better. But then the circumstances are worse than they could be because of the way they behave.

Where does power ultimately lie in the novel?
With the law of unintended consequences.

ABOUT WRITING :

When do you write?
At evenings and weekends. Not often enough.

Where do you write?
On the train home from work, or at the dinner table. On a sunny day I might take a notebook to the park. Rewriting is done at a computer screen.

Why do you write?
Because I can't paint or compose.

If you could paint or compose would you still write?
I expect that whatever I did I'd wonder if I wouldn't be happier doing something else. As a writer, I envy composers their ability to work in a medium unhampered by meanings; as a composer I'd probably wish I could do more than arrange these patterns of sounds.

How do you start?
Usually I've had an idea in the back of my head for months. It might be a fully worked out scene, or hardly more than an atmosphere. Finally I run out of excuses.

Do you have any writing rituals?
No, but I'm becoming increasingly fetishistic about pens.

Who or what inspires you?
Emulation/competition with other, more prolific writers. And a sense of time running out.

What do you read if you need a prompt?
Sometimes, if, say, I've reached chapter five and am stuck, I might pick another novel at random and read its chapter five, as if to remind myself how other writers have managed. Sometimes this helps; sometimes I just end up reading chapters six and seven and then I have to stop myself.

Do you listen to music as you write? If so, do you have a favourite piece you write to?
No – it's too distracting. Though if I'm typing a handwritten draft – a more mechanical procedure – I will listen to more-or-less raucous pop, Tom Waits or Rasputina or QueenAdreena, or whoever is a favourite that month. I don't keep up. Rammstein make good typing music.

Do you use visual prompts?
Does gazing out of the window count?

Do you revise and edit your work as you go?
Yes, at every stage. If I start with a handwritten draft I make changes to that before typing it. I'll then make changes – usually deletions – as I type. Once it's on the computer I'll make more changes. Then I print it out with wide margins and make more changes, usually on the train from work. Then I type up the changes. Then there's another onscreen revision, followed by another printout and more work on the train. And so on.

What tips would you give to aspiring writers?
Be prepared to discard things: adjectives, sentences, paragraphs, chapters, entire drafts – along with any hope of leading a normal life.

What distracts you from writing?
Almost anything. If there isn't a distraction to hand I'll sometimes go and look for one.

What single thing would improve your writing life?
Being less easily distracted.

MORE FROM MYRIAD EDITIONS

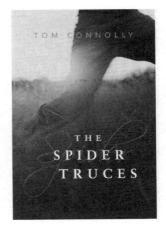

Set during the first Australian cricket tour of England in 1868, this magnificent novel explores an extraordinary friendship between Brippoki, one of the Aboriginal players, and Sarah, a bookish spinster living in London.

Sarah's quiet routine takes on a new aspect when the cricketer enlists her help to uncover the mysteries of his ancestry. From Lord's cricket ground to Greenwich's Royal Observatory and the banks of the Thames at Shadwell, they follow the trail of Joseph Druce, a convicted felon transported to New South Wales eighty years earlier.

Taking its lead from true historical events, this powerful novel, brimming with memorable characters and historical intrigue, brings Victorian London to life.

ISBN: 978-0-9562515-0-3

Against the vividly described background of 1980s rural Kent, this moving portrait of a father-son relationship shifts effortlessly between evoking utterly convincingly the terrors and joys of adolescence and the pleasure and pain of being an adult.

Ellis is obsessed by the spiders that inhabit the family's crumbling house – and also by a need to find out more about his mother, whose death overshadows the family's otherwise happy existence.

From early attempts at relationships, to unskilled jobs, flatshares and drug-addled nights on the beach, what endures is the strength of Ellis's bond with his dad – an ex-Merchant Navy man who bottles up his grief, refusing to talk about his lost wife.

ISBN: 978-0-9562515-2-7

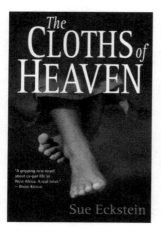

"One of those brilliant books that offers an easy, entertaining read in the first instance, only to worm its way deeper into your mind. A modern Graham Greene – fabulous...fictional gold."
Argus

"Graham Greenish with a bit of Alexander McCall Smith thrown in, very readable, a charming first novel...very humorous."
Radio 5 Live Up All Night

"Entertaining and rewarding... an excellent début. If you like Armistead Maupin, Graham Greene or Barbara Trapido, you will love this."
bookgroup.info

"Populated by a cast of miscreants and misfits this is a darkly comic delight."
Choice

ISBN: 978-0-9549309-8-1

"Skilfully evokes the era and the slow-moving quality of childhood summers, suggesting the menace lurking just beyond the vision of her young protagonists. A study of memory and guilt with several twists."
Guardian

"This emotionally charged thriller grips from the first paragraph, and a nail-biting level of suspense is maintained throughout. A great second novel."
She

"Such is the vividness of the descriptions of the location in this well structured and well written novel that I want to get the next train down. On the edge of my seat? No way – I was cowering under it."
shotsmag.co.uk

ISBN: 978-0-9549309-4-3

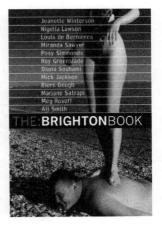

"An exquisitely crafted début novel set in a post-apocalyptic landscape. I'm rationing myself to five pages per day in order to make it last."
Guardian Unlimited

"An all-too-convincing picture of life...in the middle of this century – cold and stormy, with most modern conveniences long-since gone, and with small, mainly self-sufficient, communities struggling to maintain a degree of social order. It is very atmospheric...leaves an indelible imprint on the psyche."
BBC Radio 4 Open Book

"A decidedly original tale. Psychologically sophisticated, it demands our attention. Ignore it, O Philistines, at your peril."
bookgroup.info

ISBN: 978-0-9549309-2-9

"*The Brighton Book* is a fantastic idea and I loved writing a piece with crazy wonderful Brighton as the theme. Everybody should buy the book because it's such a great mix of energy and ideas."
Jeanette Winterson

"Packed with unique perspectives on the city...*The Brighton Book* has hedonism at its heart. Give a man a fish and you'll feed him for a day. Give him *The Brighton Book* and you will feed him for a lifetime."
Argus

A celebration of Brighton and Brightonians – resident, itinerant and visiting – in words and pictures, with original contributions from Piers Gough, Lenny Kaye, Nigella Lawson, Woodrow Phoenix, Meg Rosoff, Jeanette Winterson and others.

ISBN: 978-0-9549309-0-5

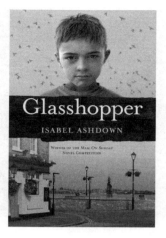

"Tender and subtle, it explores difficult issues in deceptively easy prose...Across the decades, Ashdown tiptoes carefully through explosive family secrets. This is a wonderful debut – intelligent, understated and sensitive."
Observer

"An intelligent, beautifully observed coming-of-age story, packed with vivid characters and inch-perfect dialogue. Isabel Ashdown's storytelling skills are formidable; her human insights highly perceptive."
Mail on Sunday

"Isabel Ashdown's first novel is a disturbing, thought-provoking tale of family dysfunction, spanning the second half of the 20th century, that guarantees laughter at the uncomfortable familiarity of it all."
'Best Books of the Year', *London Evening Standard*

"An immaculately written novel with plenty of dark family secrets and gentle wit within. Recommended for book groups."
Waterstone's Books Quarterly

ISBN: 978-0-9549309-7-4